Dim light streamed through the open cellar door, and he could just make out the hole in the stone wall before the rustle of material forced him to retreat a step.

He dared not take the path back to his corner in the dark, lest he knock something over or disturb a jar. He stood, stock still, fear of discovery pressing down on his spine.

He heard the rush of breathing and the scraping of the stones. When he inched his head around the corner, he saw the outline of a woman, her dark clothes making her nearly invisible, only the soft sounds of the stones giving away her presence.

Ellie? He wanted to say the name but knew he must bide his time. Whatever she was doing, he must not startle her.

When the scraping of stones stopped, the woman retreated up the steps and lowered the cellar doors, leaving him encased in blackness once again.

S. DIONNE MOORE is a multi-published author who makes her home in Pennsylvania with her husband of twenty-one years and her daughter. You can visit her at www.sdionnemoore.com.

Books by S. Dionne Moore

HEARTSONG PRESENTS
HP912—Promise of Tomorrow
HP932—Promise of Yesterday

Promise of Time

S. Dionne Moore

Heartsong Presents

In loving memory of Jacalyn Wilcoxon, pastor's wife, friend, mentor. I miss you.

A note from the Author:
I love to hear from my readers! You may correspond with me by writing:

S. Dionne Moore
Author Relations
PO Box 721
Uhrichsville, OH 44683

ISBN 978-1-61626-285-3

PROMISE OF TIME

All scripture quotations are taken from the King James Version of the Bible.

Our mission is to publish and distribute inspirational products offering exceptional value and biblical encouragement to the masses.

PRINTED IN THE U.S.A.

one

Gettysburg, Pennsylvania, 1863

The prayer of the reverend, standing on a raised platform for all to see and hear, droned in Ellie's ears. She saw him but did not see him. Her heart and eyes focused more on the huge arch designating the entrance to Evergreen Cemetery and the rising fog that still clung over the raw mounds of dirt, marking the fresh graves in the new burial site of Gettysburg, about to be officially dedicated.

Reverend Stockton got louder, his prayer building, the words plucking at the taut chords of her heart. ". . .because Thou hast called us, that Thy blessings await us, and that Thy designs. . ."

Blessings!

Witnessing the terror of her friends and family during those terrible days of intense battle between the North and South. This was a blessing? What of the mourning Wade family, grieved over the loss of Genny, their young daughter, killed by a stray bullet as she made bread? The stench of death, still a powerful memory in her mind, when bodies lay in the fields bloated and rotting. Ellie's breath choked and she pressed her hand against her mouth. What of the *blessing* of a husband of less than two years lying in a grave in hated Southern soil, lost and forgotten except by the one person who had loved him?

". . .in reverence of Thy ways, and in accordance with Thy word, we love and magnify the infinite perfections. . ."

Ellie pressed her hand tighter to her lips. A touch on her elbow made her turn toward her friend.

"Ellie?"

She could hear the concern in Rose's voice.

"You need to rest. Why don't we go home?"

Ellie took a deep breath. She couldn't allow her own grief to pull her friend away from this very important program, not with the president set to speak. Besides, at some point she needed to distance herself from her grief if she was to be of any use to Rose. Her quiet friend's swelling body and pale face showed signs of her own private torment, what with the impending birth of her first child and the continued report of her husband missing in action.

Ellie led her friend through the crowd, mostly women. Some reached out to her, widows themselves. She felt their isolation in a physical way that pinched her vision to a narrow tunnel, and at the end of that tunnel was the cold stone of a grave marker.

Sunshine broke through the haze that marked the beginning of the day and shone down on her head, yet she felt it from a distance, the warmth unable to penetrate the shell of her grief.

"I believe we will see some sunshine today after all," Rose murmured, resting a hand on her stomach. "It will be good to feel warm again."

"Yes. It would feel good," Ellie said, more to placate her friend than from any feeling of conviction. How long had it been since she'd felt the lulling warmth of peace? Seven long months. Ever since the news came that Martin had died.

"You don't have to stay for me," Rose said.

Ellie closed her eyes and swallowed. Forced a smile. "You wanted to hear Mr. Everett. We should stay." Mr. Edward Everett's speech would be long. She knew the man's reputation, and she was unsure what reserve of strength she would draw from to survive what was surely to be a long day of even longer speeches. "And Mr. Lincoln, of course. What a treasure to have him come and speak on our behalf." She again pressed her hand to her lips, recalling the president's own recent grief.

To lose a child so young. She chided herself for being selfish. Others knew grief and still functioned. She must as well. "I—I think I'll take a stroll."

She felt Rose's eyes on her, and when her friend held out a handkerchief, Ellie took it without comment. That Rose knew where Ellie's stroll would take her didn't surprise her. The sight of row upon row of neatly placed graves tore at her. She rolled with the wave of fresh grief, shocked anew by the bitter taste of despair that sucked away what fleeting strength she had tried to cloak herself with.

She knelt at the edge of the field of graves. Disbelief swirling. All of this was a mistake. It had to be. Martin should be here, in Gettysburg, not buried haphazardly in some Southern field. She closed her eyes and went to her knees in the damp soil, uncaring of those who might be staring. No, they would have their attention fastened upon the speaker, she comforted herself. She shifted, grinding dirt into her skirts, dimly aware that the long prayer had ended and music played. She made use of Rose's handkerchief until it became a saturated mass.

The music went quiet, and a man's rich voice began the slow rise that marked the beginning of a speech. Everett. Rose must be entranced. Having heard so much of the orator and his absolute support of the Union's cause, her friend had been excited to hear him talk. Ellie caught only bits and pieces of the man's speech as she walked along the perimeter of the crowd, too restless to sit, too grieved to stand still.

Her legs had begun to ache when a smattering of applause broke her reverie. Ellie headed back toward the place where she had parted from Rose. Thousands of people crowded around the raised platform. When Ellie could not discern the familiar shape of her friend, panic plucked at her. Rose wouldn't leave her. She was sure of it. Her throat closed. Maybe something terrible had happened. Dread squeezed her chest. She would be alone. Again.

Ellie took in the smear of pale faces staring her way. One moved in her direction and touched her arm. "Are you all right, ma'am?"

She did not recognize the man, nor the woman beside him. A couple. She squeezed her eyes shut and shook her head.

"Ellie?"

Rose!

She turned, and Rose's small form hurried toward her. "I was keeping an eye out for you." Concern etched Rose's expression and dimmed the twinkle in her eyes. "You've been crying."

"I'm fine."

Ellie could see the protest form on Rose's lips, but she turned her attention back to the speaker, steeling herself. She did her best to concentrate on the speech, but only when President Lincoln stood did she feel anything close to anticipation. Here was the man—black crepe around his top hat in honor of the death of his own son—who understood death in a personal way. President Lincoln's presence injected a measure of life into the corner of her heart that the news of Martin's death had withered.

Papers in hand, his higher-pitched voice strong with conviction, Lincoln began. "Fourscore and seven years ago. . ."

❧

Theodore watched from the shadows of Rupp's Tannery as a group of men on horseback cantered down Baltimore Street, passed him, then eased onto Emmitsburg Road. He pressed his back to the building that squatted parallel to Baltimore Street and prayed the moonlight would not reveal him. He withdrew to the back of the building, crossed the yard, forged a small stream, and passed through several yards before he reached Breckinridge Street. He stared at the house in front of him. It was the one he remembered from the day of his cousin's marriage. His cousins's bride's house, left to her by her mother. The place Theo hoped to find her.

His tension eased when he realized the windows of the brick house were dark. A wide oak tree blocked the front of the house from view, but his cousin's letters had described the clever entry to a cellar at one end of the porch and how his wife worked hard at putting up vegetables and storing various canned goods in the cool space. It was the place he hoped to call home for the night.

Theo rested against the cold brick and dared to close his eyes. His feet burned with rawness, a torture worsened with every passing day but endured out of necessity. He dared not loose the bloody strips of cloth he had tied on to relieve the pain in his bare feet.

In slow degrees, his body relaxed, but he jerked alert in the next breath. Exhaustion would be his downfall. He pushed himself away from the brick wall and went to his hands and knees. With ears keen from nights spent discerning the difference between the sounds of humans or animals approaching, Theo absorbed the atmosphere. Where his vision might fail, his ears would not.

Satisfied that nothing out of the ordinary moved, he stood and hastened toward the house. Sweat broke out on his upper lip as the porch came into view. He squeezed himself up close to the brick wall of his cousin's house and slithered toward the porch. In the darkness, he felt for the hinges of the cellar door and found the ring used to pull the door open.

Theo spit into his hand and smeared the wetness on first the top hinge then the lower one and prayed the added moisture would work as a lubricant and keep the door from squeaking. With trepidation, he eased the door toward him, drawing a breath only when the opening became large enough for him to slip through.

With the door firmly shut behind him, he felt his way along with his hands, a damp, cool wall of stone greeting his fingertips and scrubbing his palms. For a moment he stood perplexed. The porch ran the length of the house, a good ten feet by his estimate, yet he guessed that he had come only five feet. This stone wall must be to support the middle section to avoid sag. Sure his assessment must be correct, he followed the wall into a room that smelled of apples, with undertones of dust and mildew. But the cool air refreshed him. He longed for a light to see by but dared not risk giving himself away, even if he did possess a lantern.

His fingers skimmed the jars of produce and rough gunnysacks of apples and potatoes. Food. His hand closed around the smooth skin of an apple, and he sank his teeth into the fruit, surprised by the tart bite of the tender flesh. He munched as quietly as he could then began on a potato and finished with another apple.

A dull thud brought him up straight. His hands went clammy and he lowered the apple and cocked his head to listen harder.

The sound did not repeat. He took another bite, quieter this time. It must be someone in the house turning over in bed or falling out. If Martin's wife, Ellie, was not alone, or if she had relatives living with her in the wake of her grief, his chances of being identified increased. The thought congealed the contents of his stomach into a heaving mass.

He put the apple aside and stretched out on the dirt floor, his body demanding rest. With his fist, he made a pillow of a small sack of apples. He closed his eyes and tried to plan how he would introduce himself into the household.

What would Ellie Lester be like in person? He had read so much about her in Martin's letters that Theo felt as if he knew her. But among Martin's personal effects, he never located a picture. Not everyone, he supposed, had the benefit of such a treasure to remember a loved one by, but he had hoped to remind himself what she looked like before coming face-to-face with her. His cousin's wedding to the woman had been a long time ago, and though Theo recalled the day, the faces had receded a bit as the horrors of war had driven the pleasant memories into hiding.

Something tickled along Theo's arm, and he slapped at the place, feeling the crush of a tiny body. A spider, no doubt. With a weary sigh, he rolled to his side and fell into a deep sleep.

two

Ellie tied a dark handkerchief over her golden hair. She crossed to the table and tested the knot of the dishcloth, in which she had tied a loaf of bread and cold salt meat from her lone supper. Rose had invited her to stay and eat with her, but Ellie had made the decision to seclude herself after the dedication ceremony to rest for the evening duties she needed to perform. Though she made sure to remind Rose to call her should her labor begin.

"You know I will."

"The minute your pain starts," Ellie pressed.

Rose had given her a wan smile. "The very minute."

Her friend's pale complexion had concerned Ellie, but she knew little of babies and birthing. She would be the one to go fetch Martha, the black woman who had attended more births than Ellie could count.

Ellie leaned forward and tested the weight of the food within the dishcloth. Too heavy and she would have a hard time slipping quickly down the cellar stairs. She peered out her darkened kitchen window and waited, her ears attuned to the ticking clock and the chimes to mark two o'clock in the morning. It would be soon, she knew. She moved back to the table and sat, her hands cupping the package of food. She inhaled the familiar scents of fresh linen combined with that of fried salt pork that still lingered.

She loved her home, left to her—along with the family farm on the outskirts of Gettysburg—upon the death of her mother. Her only regret—that she could not have shared it with Martin for more than the few months they had been

12

together. Her mother's death, followed so closely by Martin's, compounded her sadness. Still, she had a home, and her mother's words echoed in her head. *"A woman should have a place of her own, Ellie, and there's no place like your birthplace."*

Ellie couldn't help the smile. Her mother might have been gentle and kind, but she also had a backbone made of brick. After her death, Ellie had moved back into town, renting the farmhouse to a young couple and the land to a farmer to work.

This house suited her better than the farm. She loved the uniqueness of the building—two separate homes under one roof, the front porch shared by both—and having Rose so close by. She had been thrilled when Martin agreed to stay in town versus moving out to the farm, especially when talk of war had started to brew.

Oh, Martin.

The clock began to chime the hour, and Ellie snapped from her memories and got to her feet. She hefted the dishcloth of food and stepped out into the night. She was careful to watch where she placed her feet, the ends of the boards less squeaky than the centers. But too close to the edge and a warped board might groan a protest. She breathed more easily when she cleared the porch and made her way to the cellar as fast as she could.

She hesitated when the cool air of the cellar whooshed across her face and neck. Something didn't seem quite right. She held the door and squinted into the darkness. As far as she could see, the stone wall in front of her remained intact, so no worries there. That's when it came to her. The door. Of course. She wiggled the door back and forth and realized it hadn't uttered its normal whine of protest. Perhaps the wood had dried a bit in the low humidity and shrunk enough to solve the problem.

Ellie shrugged off the matter and descended the cellar steps until she stood in front of the stone wall that supported the porch in the middle. She began to work at the loose stones with her bare fingers then searched in her apron pocket for the slender knife she carried for such purposes. Removing the first stone was always the most difficult. With the aid of the knife, she wedged the tip between a gap and withdrew the first stone. The smell of unwashed bodies hit her full in the face. When five stones were removed, she set the dishcloth on the ledge, turned her back on the hole, and marched up the steps to the yard where she shrank beneath a tree.

In the dim light, the man and two women moved from the cover of the cellar toward the back of the house.

As fast as she could, Ellie returned to the cellar and replaced the stones. In the stillness of the night, she could see nothing moving. She didn't know where the runaways escaped to. It was safer that way.

"Lord, go with them," she whispered.

&

Theo's heart rate slowed with each passing minute of silence. Again, his ears had not failed him even though his body lay suspended in near unconsciousness. At first his instinct had been to rise and run, but the darkness of the cellar had registered in his mind and assured him that whoever he was hearing could not see him.

He had gone to his knees and crawled from his corner toward the doorway. Sounds of scratching and stabbing against a rough surface made him hold his breath. He heard more scraping then light steps retreating. He weighed whether he should retreat to the tree in the front yard or stay put.

But as he debated, more noises came to his ears. This time a lower murmur—a grunt. A low sniff. A pair of footsteps on the stairs, then another, and another, the tread of the last heavier than the first two. A wave of fetid, warm air assaulted Theo's nose. He stood to his feet, biting down on a gasp as his tender feet were reintroduced to his full weight.

Dim light streamed through the open cellar door, and he could just make out the hole in the stone wall before the rustle of material forced him to retreat a step. He dared not take the path back to his corner in the dark, lest he knock something over or disturb a jar. He stood, stock still, fear of discovery pressing down on his spine.

He heard the rush of breathing and the scraping of the stones. When he inched his head around the corner, he saw the outline of a woman, her dark clothes making her nearly invisible, only the soft sounds of the stones giving away her presence.

Ellie? He wanted to say the name but knew he must bide his time. Whatever she was doing, he must not startle her.

When the scraping of stones stopped, the woman retreated up the steps and lowered the cellar doors, leaving him encased in blackness once again.

three

Theo lay still, wide awake yet confused. He longed for a watch of some sort to tell the time and free him from the prison of not knowing how long he slept or whether it was day or night. He rubbed his head and scratched his chest. A bath would be nice. A real bath. Not a little bit of water on an already filthy rag, but one with warm water and a bar of soap.

Theo groaned and lay back on the earthen floor of the cellar, feeling very much a prisoner of a different sort than the ones the army demanded. He grinned and reached under his head for the sack and withdrew an apple. At least he would not go hungry, surrounded as he was by the store of vegetables.

His first bite of the fruit did nothing to alleviate his ever-darkening mood. Mushy on his tongue, the apple was one best used for sauces or apple butter than for snacking. Eating presented another problem as his system awakened to the presence of food. He finished off the apple and sank back against the sack. He would go mad in this darkness.

With renewed determination, he got to his feet and felt his way to the doorway. Each step brought him closer to the place where the cellar began. It took a minute for him to realize the blackness had receded somewhat and that he could vaguely make out the stone wall he had seen the previous night. When he turned his head in the direction of the cellar stairs, he saw the strips of daylight through the cracks in the doors.

His heart rejoiced at the prospect of sunlight and fresh air. Of an outhouse. He had to do something and knew he would be able to judge by the place of the sun in the sky what time of day it was.

Before he could climb the first step, something scraped against the outside of the doors. As fast as his sore feet would allow, he hobbled back to his spot and realized his first duty should have been to find a way to hide himself rather than to feed his stomach.

The doors swung open and streams of light bounced off the stone wall. He stood stock still, unsure what to do or what to say, for surely the woman was not returning to release more runaway slaves from their hiding place. Not at this time of day. If it was a woman, she would scream upon seeing him, and he couldn't afford that.

Able to see the interior of the room now, Theo crouched near the doorway. The whooshing of skirts and petticoats confirming the gender of his visitor.

He picked up a potato lying in a neat pile and gripped it in his fist. When he figured the woman would be ready to round the corner, he rolled the potato along the floor in her path, hoping to divert her attention and give himself time to come up behind her.

Her gasp and squeal let him know the ruse had worked. He poked his head around the corner. Her face was turned in the direction of the potato. In an instant he was behind her and pressing his palm over her mouth.

She tensed.

"Don't scream. Please. I can explain, and I'm not going to hurt you."

He hated the fear he was generating and continued to speak in a soothing voice even as his nerves burned. If she got away, if he let go without securing her promise, he knew the consequences he would face.

"My name is Theodore Lester. We've met before. At your wedding. I'm the Southern cousin whose idea it was to hang your wedding bed from the rafters." He gulped and felt the heat creep into his cheeks, but his candor was rewarded and the terror in her expression melted into wariness.

She nodded.

He held his breath as he released his grip on her mouth and backed up two steps to give her room and a measure of reassurance that his intentions were noble. He grimaced at the irony of the thought. As noble as the intentions of a man hiding in a cellar could be.

"The name is familiar." Her words were guarded. "Martin's cousin."

"You're Ellie."

Her voice came out strained. "What are you doing here? And why didn't you come to the house instead of. . ."

He saw the moment the enormity of his problem sunk into her consciousness.

"You're a—a soldier."

Theo nodded. "Confederate, and they'll likely kill me if they find me."

❧

Ellie studied the man closely, afraid to believe he was who he said he was and afraid not to believe it. The man was admitting to being a deserter. And kin. But he was also the enemy, and she would not soon forget the conceited and bullying ways in which the Confederates had strutted about Gettysburg during its occupation. Horror stories whirled in her head, not to mention the rumors of the way the men had raided other towns for food, with little thought for the people from whom they had taken.

Yet his lean face and painfully thin frame lent credence to his story. If he had run away, he had been running for a long time. Her gaze swept the length of him, and she frowned at his feet and the sight of blood that saturated the rags that bound them.

When she raised her face to his, a horrible dread swept over her. She had come down to the cellar yesterday morning for potatoes, and last night, too, though she had not entered the cellar, just the hallway long enough to—

The thought exploded in her mind. If he had been here last night, surely he would have seen what she had been up to. She willed herself to remain calm. Not to jump to conclusions. He could have found the cellar at any time in the predawn. But the question remained. "Why here? What do you want? Why shouldn't I turn you over to the authorities?"

He drew air into his lungs, seeming to draw on some deep-seated reserve of strength.

When his gaze caressed her face then fell to the ground, her senses knotted, and for a moment she felt the first stirrings of sympathy. But his words, when he finally spoke, crushed the soft feeling beneath its heel.

"Because being a Southern gentleman, I would mightily despise telling others what your nighttime occupation involves."

four

Ellie shifted her arm so the jar of preserves nestled more firmly against the crook of her elbow. She spewed a stream of air at the still dangling strand of hair tickling her right eye, cast an eye over the cellar doors to make sure they were shut, and marched toward the house with a million thoughts ricocheting around her brain.

The memory of her wedding day was sharp in her mind. Martin's crooked grin when he saw her, the light in his eyes when he leaned in to kiss her, their late supper together, both too nervous to eat much of anything. But the faces of the guests were hazier. She remembered Theodore more because of Martin's talk of his letters and their childhood together. And, of course, the bed incident. She would make sure to take a light with her next time. She wanted to see him and make sure the man was not an imposter bent on wickedness.

Instead of heading into her side of the house, she went to the door on the other side of the long porch and gave a light knock before entering. Laid out as a mirror image to her home, Ellie had no problem finding the kitchen where Rose stirred up a panful of gravy.

"It's a beautiful morning," Ellie said, making an effort to quell her nerves and force a note of cheer that she did not feel.

"You brought the preserves?" Rose gave a glance over her shoulder, a smile lighting her hazel eyes.

"Don't I always bring something?" She bit down on her tongue. The question sounded harsh, even to her own ears. "I mean,"—she forced a light tone—"what kind of neighbor would I be if I didn't bring something to add to the meals you so kindly invite me to?"

Rose patted her hands into a mound of flour and began kneading a trough of dough. "You're always welcome."

She set the preserves on the counter at Rose's elbow.

"Peach will go well with the sourdough," Rose said.

"I need to get down in the cellar and do some organizing before next year's harvest creates more confusion. It's full of cobwebs, too, and needs a good cleaning."

"True enough." Rose's eyes twinkled. "You always come over with some manner of dust or dirt clinging to you." Her friend's eyes were on her hair, and Ellie touched the spot that held Rose's attention. She pulled out the clinging remnants of a cobweb.

"Once I get this bread to rising, we'll eat and I'll help you tackle that cellar."

"No!" She almost choked on that syllable. She forced calmness into her tone and tilted her head to indicate Rose's swollen stomach. "You shouldn't be going up and down those steps in your condition."

Rose laughed and the paleness of her complexion benefited from the exercise, bringing spots of color to her cheeks. She smoothed a hand over her midsection, a soft smile curving her pink lips. "I'm feeling fine. Never better."

"Then work on the nursery or that blanket you've been so furiously knitting. Going up and down the stairs is best left to those of us who can see our feet."

Her friend gave a mock grimace. "But look at what I'll have to show for it." Her eyes flashed to Ellie's and she gasped. "Oh, Ellie, I didn't mean for it to sound like that."

It was a fact that no children would be in her future now that Martin lay dead somewhere in the South. Maybe never. She sent her friend a smile. "I'll simply enjoy spoiling your girl."

"Boy," Rose corrected.

Ellie laughed. "Twins."

Rose chuckled and dug deeper into the dough, turning it and pushing outward. "I'll make sure to have a good dinner waiting for you when you're done down there."

"I'll set the table."

Rose swept her hands together and loosed a white cloud of flour into the air. "While you're doing that, I'll slice the ham."

Ellie did her best to put her heart into the breakfast conversation. It was times like this, when the deeds of the night before seemed to hang heavy in her mind—along with the fear that Rose might have seen or heard something—that Ellie felt most tense. And now she had yet another secret to shield from her friend.

When she finally excused herself and got the cleaning rags and broom from her own house along with a lantern, she dragged everything through the yard and around to the front of the house that faced the street, alert for prying eyes of curious neighbors. At the cellar, she put the broom against the wall and the lantern on the ground and pulled open the cellar door. She skirted down the steps of the cellar, making a racket as she went. When she reached the landing, she set the things aside and went back up the steps to retrieve the rest. When she finally pulled the doors closed behind her, darkness engulfed her and a shiver went up her spine.

≈

Theo heard the telltale rattle of the cellar doors and swept to his feet as icy dread suffused him. He lunged toward the doorway and picked up a potato, bent on distracting the person as he had done with Ellie. His only option—to give himself time to escape.

Lord, please let it be Ellie.

When he thought the person close, he rolled the potato through the doorway and bit his lip.

"Do you honestly think I'd fall for that again?"

Ellie. Relief flooded him, and he staggered backward and collapsed. She appeared with all manner of things in her arms. Though he wished to rise and help her, he knew his legs would not hold him.

"Theo?" Concern etched her tone. He heard the strike of a match and watched as she lit the wick of a lantern then lowered the chimney.

Shadows fell back and still he felt the weakness, ashamed of it. "You scared me."

She held the lantern up and crossed to him. In the light he could make out her features. The same woman he had seen right before the war. Martin's bride. Then she had been flushed with life and hope for her future with Martin. Now the blue of her eyes held shadows, and her expression seemed weighted by the cares and horrors she had experienced in the interim.

"We'll need to set up a signal of some sort so that you'll know when it's me coming."

Her words brought him a measure of relief. "Are you ill?" She placed the lantern on a low ledge and sunk down beside him. Her cool hand pressed against his forehead.

He tried to form an answer but could not. He jerked his head away from her touch and closed his eyes. "Nothing food wouldn't solve. I'm sick of apples and raw potatoes."

For a golden moment, her laugh encased him in a bubble of warmth. "I didn't think to bring anything from the last meal." She paused and her brow creased. "I'll have to figure something out."

He knew the question he was about to ask seemed pathetic, but he had to ask it for his own sanity. "You won't tell on me?"

Her lips firmed and her gaze met his, unflinching. "If you promise not to reveal what you saw."

Theo nodded, content in their stalemate. He had made the threat of telling about her night occupations out of desperation. He could never do something so terrible to a lady, and especially not to the wife of his cousin, but she didn't know that. Let her think him a cad. He had little choice. "Do you keep them every night?" he asked.

She sat back on her heels, her skirts puffed slightly around her. A lone minute passed as her eyes seemed to focus on the bandages on his feet. She reached out her hand as if to touch the soiled rags. "No. There was a problem and they had to come here. For that reason, I was thinking it would be a good place for you." She raised her head. "Before you decide to move on."

He recognized the steel that had inserted itself into her tone. He was not to let himself get too comfortable in her home and think he could stay.

"I'll bring some salve for your feet and bind them with clean linen." In a smooth action, she got to her feet and brushed at the dirt on her skirts. "For now, I've work to do."

She moved about the room, rag in hand, kicking up a cloud of dust that tickled his throat. He did his best to keep his eyes elsewhere but would inevitably find himself drawn to her form.

Bits and pieces of his cousin's wedding day came into focus. Martin's laughter that precluded his usual tendency toward stoicism. It had not been hard to see that Ellie's good-natured personality had drawn Martin out of his shell. Theo recalled, again, the way Martin had talked of her in his letters, with pride and love.

He wanted to tell her what he had seen. Of Martin's last moments. Such knowledge would ease her grief but generate a very different pain. That of betrayal. Now that he had seen her, he wondered if telling her the truth was merely his excuse to fly toward freedom or his misplaced sense of duty toward his cousin. If he told her all he knew and handed over the mementos he had secured, there would be no lasting reason for him to stay, and he would be on the run again.

He closed his eyes and licked his lips. He wanted so much

to rest. To be strong again, whole and happy. Unhindered by war and death, friendships cut short by shrapnel or balls or bullets.

Just a little while. I'll rest. Then I'll tell her all I know and move on.

five

It galled Ellie to see him lie there, unresponsive and uncaring, while she was working so hard to clean the cellar. Martin would have certainly asked by now, and even if she had turned down his offer of help, he would have done something else to ease her burden. It was the kind of man her husband had been.

When Ellie sneaked another peek at Theo, she was again struck by the evidence of his weariness. The same telltale marks that she'd seen in the soldiers she'd helped nurse back to health in the wake of the Battle of Gettysburg. Dark circles. Paleness. A strange sensitivity. She'd heard stories from Union soldiers of Rebels stealing boots off dead bodies. Of their strange screeching yell that invaded their nightmares.

Yet she had tended Confederate soldiers as well and knew that they suffered just as much as the ones they called their enemies. Perhaps more so. Most were more poorly dressed than the Union soldiers. And when they would ask for the result of the battle and learned of Lee's retreat, a fierceness seemed to overtake them. Or complete resignation.

Theo's feet, bound in bloody, old rags, seemed to speak to her of horrors she could not comprehend. Was it so bad that he had to escape? She had no doubt that he had walked hundreds of miles, spent nights hiding in the woods, and it struck her that the runaways she aided probably had it better than a deserter.

Martin's letters spoke of scanty provisions and long marches, but the letters he wrote did not often linger on the atrocities of war. He might allude to something, but he would always smooth it over by sharing something funny or personal, a dream he had for them when they were reunited or the memory of a private moment that never failed to draw a smile from her.

Seeing Theo's face had assured her he was who he said he was, though he was slimmer and the boyish curves of his face had matured into angular planes since their last meeting. His eyes were the same. As soon as the lantern light revealed his silver-gray eyes, it pulled up a clear memory from her wedding day. That of Martin's cousin standing in the doorway of the barn with the bed dangling high above his head. Those eyes shining bright with mischief as Martin howled with laughter.

She placed her rag over the bristles of the broom and lifted it to clear a cobweb in the corner of the room. As she continued working, she knew that Martin would want her to help Theo, even to hide him.

Her arms grew weary of the dusting, and she stopped to survey her work, satisfied with what she saw. She turned when a low groan issued from behind her.

Theo writhed on the floor like a man in deep pain.

She went to him and pressed her hand to his cheek. He jerked and the motion startled her back on her heels. She grabbed his shirt to gain leverage, but the thin material rent beneath her touch. She sat down hard on the dirt floor as Theo came up to a sitting position, blinking awake.

Stunned, Ellie could only stare.

In a slow movement that betrayed the depth of the slumber she'd woken him from, Theo braced his hand against the floor and stood. If his feet caused pain, his face did not show it. "I'm sorry. Let me help you up." The slow drawl of his words marked him as Southern more than his appearance.

"You were groaning terribly. I thought. . ." His hand touched her elbow and guided her upward. Her thoughts scrambled in the second that he steadied her, and she felt the intense desire to draw close to him, even if for a moment. Just to feel once again the comfort of a man's embrace. She drew in a breath and gave herself a mental shake.

His hands grasped her upper arms and set her away from him. "I sometimes have nightmares," he explained.

She turned away, confused and saddened.

❧

Theo didn't know what to do. Everything in Ellie's demeanor communicated stress. He wondered if she had been hurt in her tumble but didn't know how to ask. Ignoring the discomfort in his feet, he took up the broom she had left in the corner and began sweeping the dirt floor.

Her delicate cough caught his attention.

He stopped and looked at her through a haze of dirt.

She gave him a small smile. "You're kicking up quite a cloud of dust. You can't sweep a dirt floor like you do a wood one."

"Oh." He stared at the broom as if it alone had been the offender. "I'd offer to fetch you a cup of water, but I. . ."

"I'll get some. And some food, too." She moved to untie the apron at her waist. "You can help yourself to the peach preserves." Her gaze dipped to the tear in his shirt that revealed some skin beneath. "And a clean shirt."

He swallowed. "I need to. . ." How did a gentleman ask such a thing of a lady?

"You need to. . .what?"

"I could use a trip outside. . .to the. . .uh. . ."

Whatever she felt, it was not horror or embarrassment. Instead, her eyes crinkled at the corners and he thought he saw her nostrils flare.

"I assure you it is no laughing matter, ma'am."

This time she did laugh. "I'm sorry." He could see the effort it took for her to get serious, and the sight lightened his guilt. If she could chuckle, even at his expense, it meant she must not be hurt. "It's really dangerous for you to be out during the day. It's around back, you see, and Rose, my friend, uses that entrance far more than she uses the front. So it's a matter of timing."

"I'll do whatever it takes to keep you safe."

She went still. Her lips pressed together, and she averted her face.

He reviewed what he had said, realized the intimate suggestion of his words, and ran a hand over the back of his neck. "What I meant—"

Her gaze snapped to his. "I'll think of something. First, I'll get the food and some clothes, maybe a bucket and some soap?" Her eyes dropped to his feet. "And some salve for those feet."

She lifted her skirts and passed through the doorway and up the cellar stairs before he could make sense of anything.

Her reaction didn't seem reasonable. But having grown up with three brothers and no sisters, he doubted he would ever understand women. Down South, before war had left things in shambles, he had admired women for their beauty and poise. But he had never found a woman who could fire his mind and match his desire for conversation that did not revolve around the latest ball or beau or gossip.

Theo sat on the dirt floor and crossed his legs. No matter, he had enough muddying the waters of his life without worrying about the intricacies of a woman's mind. It might be better for him to simply tell her the terrible truth of her husband's death and move on.

six

Ellie stroked the material of Martin's shirt against her face. In searching for something that would fit Theodore, she had been unprepared for the clutch of emotion fingering Martin's shirts stirred. She could imagine the scent of him rising from the smooth fibers. When she closed her eyes, she tried to picture him at his shaving stand, hair not yet combed from the rumpled mass sleep produced, donning the shirt and working the buttons.

She yanked the shirt away from her face and balled it up. Why had he left her? Why hadn't he written to her those last months? She didn't want to be alone. A widow.

Ellie eyed the bed and debated about draping herself across it and having a good cry, but the image of Theo surfaced, his torn shirt and dirty face. His feet. He needed this shirt. She closed her eyes. How could she give something so precious to the enemy?

"Ellie?"

She turned toward the door of the bedroom and moved out onto the narrow landing. "I'm here, Rose."

"You've got mail."

Where at one time those words had struck a thrill into her heart, now she descended the stairs with more dread than hope.

Rose stood silhouetted in the kitchen, checking Ellie's bread supply then pushing into the bread box what looked to be a fresh loaf. "You need to eat more for lunch."

"I'm fine, Rose. Really."

"You hardly eat a thing, and I've held my tongue on the matter long enough." Rose's gaze sagged downward.

Ellie followed her line of vision. With a jolt, she realized she still held Martin's crumpled shirt. "I was sorting some things out to give away." Satisfied at the truth of those words, Ellie gave the shirt a sharp snap and draped it across the back of the chair. "It's time, I think."

Rose made quick work of pulling some cold ham and cheese from a basket she must have brought and laying it across slices of bread. She held the sandwich out to Ellie. "Now eat."

In order to avoid fuss, Ellie accepted the offering and set the plate on the table. "With you feeding me such a huge breakfast, there's not room left for lunch."

"I'm sure you'd like me to believe that." Rose picked up her basket. "Now I've set you up with a fresh loaf of bread. Tomorrow I'll be making some apple cinnamon bread to use up some of those apples in that cellar of yours. Be sure and bring some up before supper, and I'll set to work peeling them."

Rose went through the door and grabbed the post to brace herself as she went down the single step. She stretched her back and turned her face to the sun. "It's a good day to put hay over the carrots and parsnips."

Ellie knew how much her friend loved gardening. "I had better not catch you out there on your hands and knees thinning the spinach."

Rose gave her a mischievous grin. "Now you wouldn't expect me to make a promise I can't keep."

Ellie flinched and straightened, a new idea stirring around in her head. "I'm thinking of hiring a man to help out with hauling in the last of the garden and making repairs around the house and farm. I'm sure he would be willing to work the soil for next year."

"It's a good idea."

Energized by the solution to Theo's presence amidst two women, Ellie could barely stand still. "He can get started today. . . ."

Rose's head tilted, and she climbed back up the step that led to the back of her side of the house. "Sounds like you already have someone in mind."

Her friend's keen observation took the wind from Ellie's sails. She would have to be careful with what she said. She changed the subject. "When I come over tonight, I'll be good and hungry."

"Well, that's nice to hear." Rose paused and stared at Ellie through the screen of her door. "Try to eat your lunch before you read the mail. I think one of the letters is from your uncle."

Ellie brushed back a stray strand of hair and tightened the strings of her apron before she headed back inside. A quick glance over the names on the two envelopes proved Rose was right. Uncle Ross, her mother's brother, would once again be suggesting that she, a woman, might need help maintaining the properties since Martin's death.

The three-hundred-acre farm on the outskirts of Gettysburg had taken serious damage to the barn in the three-day battle, but the other buildings had remained mostly unscathed.

Ignoring the letter, Ellie wrapped the sandwich and loaf of fresh bread in a linen towel and placed them into a cloth-lined basket along with a ceramic jar of salve, another linen cloth, and a cake of soap. She filled a bucket with fresh water, then another, hoping anyone seeing her would think the water strictly for cleaning.

She cast an eye over all she had collected and went back upstairs. In the corner of the room, a pair of Martin's boots, almost new, collected dust. She picked them up and used her apron to clean off the dust. In a drawer, she rooted around for socks and found two pairs. She stuck them into the tops of the boots and went downstairs, satisfied that she now had everything Theo needed.

❧

Theo couldn't believe all the things Ellie had gathered in the short time she had been gone. It was the sight of the ham and cheese sandwich that brought him the greatest pleasure. He sank his teeth into the salty meat and smooth cheese and munched quietly as Ellie spread out her supplies.

"If you change quickly, I'll take you around back. Rose is probably taking her afternoon nap. She tires easily because she's expecting her first child any day. The tree shields you from the road, but wearing these clothes and agreeing to help us with some repairs and the garden would make your presence legitimate."

"Slow down there." He eyed the shirt she held up. "Won't those who meet me recognize Martin's clothes?"

She lowered her arms. It was obvious by the distress in her face that she had not anticipated such a problem, but then she held the shirt out to him. "It won't matter. I just told Rose I was going to give clothes away. It makes sense I might give the hired man first pick."

She bent over the box she had brought down. "And here." She held up a pair of fine boots. "You can probably fit into these, and I brought one of Martin's hats to keep you from being easily described to anyone who might be hunting you. Can you limp?"

He took a great gulp of the cold water she had smuggled down in the basket. "Limp," he said in a flat tone. "You want me to limp?"

"People might wonder why you haven't volunteered or been conscripted."

He eyed the boots she held out to him, the thought of stuffing his sore feet into the confines of them enough to make him think limping would not be too hard a ruse to keep up, especially if they were too small. He wolfed down the rest of the sandwich and tried one of the boots on. His foot got stuck halfway down. He pushed harder, feeling something soft. Pulling it off, he ran his hand down inside and pulled out a pair of socks.

Ellie rolled her eyes. "I forgot. I put a pair of socks in each one."

Theo tried again; this time his foot slid easily into the fine leather. They were a little bigger than he needed, but with the socks they would be almost perfect.

"We should get some salve on those feet first."

He acquiesced and pulled the boot off. He worked the bandages off slowly, wincing as the loosened scabs bled. He set about bathing his feet as Ellie continued wielding the broom over the walls.

"When I'm done, I'll leave these things down here and you can. . ."

He saw the heat of a blush in her cheeks and caught the direction of her thoughts. He needed a bath, and they both knew it. He stroked his hand over the soft wool of the shirt he held. "I can't thank you enough for the clothes."

Her chin came up. "They're Martin's. He would want you to have them."

"But you didn't have to give them to me."

"They'll keep you warm while you're here. You're probably not used to the cold."

Her tone conveyed a coolness that he found strange.

"There's a pump out back near the outhouse and tools in the building beside the garden plot."

Theo nodded, his mind spinning with all she was telling him.

"I'll leave the salve here for later, after you've plowed. I eat with Rose, but I'm sure if you take good care of her garden, she'd be delighted to offer you something to eat." She turned on her heel and snapped up the rag and broom. "It'll take me about half an hour to clean up the other room."

Other room? He thought she might be leaving until he heard the scraping sound of the previous evening and realized she was taking stones from the wall. *That* room. Theo understood that her declaration of how long it would take her was a warning for his sake as well as hers.

He made good use of the water and soap Ellie had brought down. He donned his cousin's clothes, grateful for the warmth and the cleanness of the material. Though Martin had been shorter than he by an inch and wider in the chest, they still fit well enough.

His belly full and feeling cleaner than he had in weeks, he peeked around the corner of the room and out onto the landing. Five stones had been removed to make a hole in the wall just large enough for a medium-build person to push through. He cleared his throat.

"I'm not finished yet, but we need to get you started on some work if you're to earn something to eat." He heard her skirts swishing closer and wondered how she had ever hauled herself up into that hole. She must be stronger than she looked.

When Ellie's head popped out of the hole, he held out his hand, offering help.

She shook her head. "If you'll just turn around. . ."

He presented his back and listened until he heard her land lightly on the dirt floor. "Is it safe?"

"Yes." She lifted a stone and slid it into place.

Theo followed her lead, brushing aside her help, his fingers swiping against hers. She yanked away. He finished the task, and when he glanced at her, she averted her gaze and rushed up the steps to shove open the cellar doors. She popped out of the cellar and held up her hand to indicate he should wait.

It took a minute before she came back. "Hurry, or someone might think it. . .unseemly that we were down there together." She darted into the inner room and lifted the chimney to blow out the lantern. She brushed by him, motioning for him to follow.

He emerged as fast as he could and together they shut the doors of the cellar, a low creak screeching a protest. "My first repair," he said.

She nodded and allowed him to come abreast of her. She

began to recite a short list of tasks that needed to be completed on the house, but her words slid away as he breathed the chill November air.

His shirt offered warmth. Emerging from the darkness and doing work around the place would be a welcome diversion. It was more than he could have asked for, though he knew he would have to be careful.

"Don't forget to limp," she encouraged.

"Maybe if I ball up a pair of those socks that'll help me remember."

She pursed her lips and nodded.

A wagon rattled down the road and Ellie raised her hand in response to the wagon driver's wave. Theo did the same. No time like the present to try to fit into the community.

From his scan of the area, he could see that the large oak tree in the front yard screened the front porch with its gnarled, nearly bare branches. The side of the house had a lone evergreen of some sort that provided only a brief screen when one walked from the back to the front. A small road entered the property after the tree and led to the back of the house. There he saw the remnants of the past year's harvest.

Ellie pointed to a building on the opposite side of the yard, near a gate that marked the end of the property and the beginning of the next. "Tools are in the shed. If you could turn out the horses while you're in there. . ."

He crossed the lawn, the grass brown and crunching under his feet. The smell of horseflesh came familiar and strong to him. A dappled gray and a bay mare came to see who had entered their domain. He admired the strong lines of the smaller horse and the beauty of the gray's markings.

After releasing them, he inspected the interior. A rusty hoe, a well-used shovel, a leather harness, a sidesaddle, a plow, and numerous other tools were neatly lined up along one wall. He chose what he thought he would need to get started, wishing

Ellie had at least told him more about the things grown in the garden.

"Here."

He jerked at the sound of Ellie's terse command.

She shoved a hat at him. "You should wear this. It'll help keep you from being recognized."

He nodded and put the hat on.

She stared at him, her expression unreadable. "I'll be down in the cellar if you need me."

Theo smiled into her eyes. "Am I going to get hired hand wages?"

He could tell by the stricken look on her face that she hadn't considered such a thing.

"I'll expect a good price," he poked fun at her.

Something in her expression faded, and she went pale. He thought he caught a sheen of tears in her eyes, but she hurried away before he could think of anything to say.

seven

Ellie pressed her back against the cool rocks of the cellar wall and let the tears fall, her first glimpse of Theo in Martin's clothes uppermost in her mind. When she had held the material of Martin's shirt to her cheek in the bedroom, she had felt the loneliness of his death, but seeing Theo in that same shirt gripped her with another emotion. One that beckoned her to move on. It had unnerved her almost as much as when his fingers grazed against hers, and when she'd seen him in Martin's boots. The clean scent of him and the way his too long hair curled on his neck brought a longing squeeze to her heart.

She shuddered, warming away the chill by rubbing her upper arms. To move on meant to betray the love she held for Martin, and she could not, would not, do that. She had forgone widow's black after two months, too depressed by the idea of continuing to wear the solemn color for six months or even a year. But she had never thought flippantly of moving on in her life and of loving again. She still loved Martin.

She touched the wetness on her cheek and pressed her fist against a heart that dared generate such traitorous thoughts. Tears streamed down her cheeks for all the tomorrows she would not have as a wife, a woman, a mother. Of bridal white scorched away by the black of mourning and of a noble man cut down with so much life still in him to be lived.

She gripped the broom and willed herself to move. With fervor fueled by anger at herself, she ferreted out the dark places she knew spiders were wont to hide in hopes of destroying their nests.

Theo turned at the sound of the woman's voice, his hand tilting the hat forward more, placing his face deeper in shadow.

"Ellie works fast. You must be the man she hired to help her."

The slender-framed, obviously pregnant woman in front of him could be none other than the friend Ellie had mentioned. "Reckon that's so, ma'am."

Something flickered in the woman's eyes and suspended them in time as they assessed each other. Too late, Theo realized that his deep drawl had lent itself to that knowing spark in Rose's eyes.

"Well, my name is Rose Selingrove, and you're welcome to have some supper with Ellie and me. You have a place around here?"

A direct question. He cast about for a way to answer that would not raise more questions. "Yes, in Ellie's cellar," was out of the question. Yet he could not truthfully say he had a place in town, which also troubled him because to say less than that would surely raise more questions and perhaps get her suspicions aroused. He shrugged. "I manage fine."

"Which probably means you don't eat very well. Men don't often eat well unless they have a woman to cook for them." She pressed a hand against her rounded belly.

"No ma'am, I guess we don't." There he went again, answering with the drawl that would peg him as Southern. He swallowed, hoping the woman might not have noticed.

Rose's smile was soft, and she took a step closer to him and stared him straight in the eyes. "With that heavy Southern accent, you're better off staying quiet. If people hear you talking like that, you just might find yourself facing a firing squad." Without missing a beat, she pointed at a row of the garden. "This row needs a smattering of hay to insulate it against the cold."

And with not another word, she spun on her heel and

marched back to the house. A collision of dread roiled his stomach, mixed with a healthy dose of respect for the woman's verve. That she hadn't reacted with horror and hysterics over the realization that he was a Southerner gave him courage. Perhaps she would be a woman he could trust. If she ran slaves, as Ellie did, wouldn't that mean she would be sympathetic by nature? And might not some of that sympathy be reserved for men like him? Even if the enemy?

She was his enemy as well, he sought to remind himself. Harboring slaves, the rightful property of their owners. He could not believe his cousin's wife would be engaged in such a practice, but what did he really expect? The North was staunch in its support of freedom for slaves, despite the expense the Southern plantation holders paid to purchase the blacks as workers.

Theo picked up a handful of straw and let it fall through his fingers. It twisted and spun its way to the ground, insulating the row as Rose had requested. He just hoped it was enough, though he was certain she would let him know if it wasn't. In the South, no one had to insulate anything against the cold. Though he'd become used to the cooler temperatures in the four months since his desertion, the winds stung him the deepest. Harsh and icy cold, they had left him a shivering mass on many nights during his journey north. But it had been a small price to pay to be free of the war. Or as free as he could be as a deserter.

He frowned down at the row of straw he had placed. Deserter seemed such an unkind word, the punishment for deserting so harsh in light of the horrors each man was made to suffer and endure. His familiar nightmares tried to niggle at him. If only he could sleep through one night without tasting the terror anew, or hearing the screams. . . .

Theo pivoted, his heel grinding into the soft dirt. He stooped to collect the tools, determined not to let the horrors of it all destroy what he had at this moment. A trembling began along his arms and into his hands. He leaned the tools against the wall of the barn and stared at his shaking, sweaty palms.

He tried to think of the list Ellie had given him, anything to block the tormenting images. *Lord, please help me.* He took a deep breath, then another, forcing his mind to the horses and the pleasure of riding one over the fields and down the roads. . . .

His hands stilled, and when he shut the door to the shed, he realized the sun skimmed the horizon in the west. He lifted his nose to the air and sniffed. It smelled of rain and something frying, and he guessed supper must not be far off. He wasn't sure if he should return to the cellar or knock on Rose's door. *Rose.*

He needed to talk to Ellie. Tell of his meeting with Rose. If Ellie deemed her friend trustworthy, he would be safe. If not. . .

He didn't want to consider it.

eight

Ellie thought fear must smell much like the long, narrow room on the other side of the stone wall in the cellar. As those people given into her care left the small enclosure, it seemed the odor clung to them as it had all the room's previous occupants. She hated that they had to live like this. To hide and endure the stress of being found out or of putting those who cared for them into danger.

Ellie figured it must be early evening. Her stomach twisted with hunger and she realized, too late, that her ham and cheese sandwich had gone untouched. At least by her. If Rose asked her about lunch she would have to change the subject quickly to avoid telling a lie.

She put a hand to her back and bent backward to ease the ache lodged tight against her spine. In short order, she had gathered all the things she'd brought down to the cellar and emptied the buckets of the dirty water.

She needed to settle Theo into a comfortable corner of the barn. Tonight would be as good a time as any to move him there. He could not hunker in her cellar. Should Rose get brave enough to negotiate the steps, she would wonder why the stranger stayed hunkered in a dark, damp cellar. She would then be forced to tell her friend all about Theo's background, a risk she really didn't want to take.

She worried over the idea as she gathered her skirts and peeked out through the hole and toward the cellar doors. No one was there. She sat and slid her left foot out first, searching with her toes for the floor of the landing before she shifted her weight, ducked her head, and pulled out of the hole. Before her toes could find the solid promise of the dirt floor, she felt a hand on her arm and gasped.

"You really should come out headfirst. It's dangerous to do it this way. Anyone could sneak up on you."

Ellie pulled her leg back up, embarrassed at exposing the naked length. She pulled herself upright and into the secret room. Theo's head popped through the opening, his grin bringing a rush of heat to her face. "Wh—where did you come from?"

"Right there." He pointed to the inner room of the cellar.

"A gentleman would never have spied on me."

His grin only widened. "Wasn't spying. I thought it best to show you the danger." His head disappeared. "I'll turn my back."

She heard the amusement in his voice and it nettled her. She had known her exit was not the best way, but it was the only way she could think of, and now she had this smirking Rebel exposing her fear and ogling what she never intended to be ogled.

She knelt and stared out the hole. True to his word, he stood with his back to her. As quick as she could, she went through the hole.

"You finished? I'm getting hungry, and the smell coming from Rose's house is tantalizing."

He faced Ellie as the words spilled over her, stilling the beat of her heart. He must have read the startled question in her eyes.

"She came out and introduced herself. I'm invited to eat with the family."

"Rose?"

"Her, too."

"No. I mean Rose invited you. . . ." She was babbling and she knew it. She drew air into her lungs and tried to settle herself. "She came out and saw you?"

"Recognized my accent, too."

Ellie berated herself for that. Why hadn't she considered that his accent would be a sure giveaway? She pursed her lips and met his gaze. Why, for that matter, hadn't *he* realized the danger of talking in front of enemies? It was his hide after all.

But she must remember how much Theo meant to Martin. The two had grown up together, until his uncle had bought a small farm in the South and moved his family. She still remembered Martin's immense satisfaction when Theo had written to say he would be traveling north to attend their wedding. While she had her head wrapped around last-minute details, Theo had spirited away Martin.

"Don't you realize how dangerous it is for people to know you're from the South?"

He shrugged.

She folded her arms. "You want me to risk my life hiding you, yet you're not caring one wit to help conceal the fact that you're a deserter from the South?"

He frowned. "I do care. I just don't know how to talk any other way."

True enough. What could she expect? His years in the South had erased whatever Northern accent he'd had as a youth. "Can't you try?"

"I could try."

There now. His words held as much Northern-ness as hers. She relaxed, the tension in her shoulders melting away. "Say something else."

"You're looking quite lovely this evening, ma'am."

His thick Southern accent caressed every syllable, and the twinkle in his eyes baited her to protest. "You're insufferable."

"No, Martin was insufferable. I'm charming."

Hearing Martin's name crushed the lighthearted moment. She ran her finger over her face to find a stray hair that tickled at her cheek, groping for something to say. "I'm moving you into the toolshed."

"The barn?"

She glared up at him. Why was he being so difficult? "Barn, toolshed, whatever you want to call it."

"The garden work will be done tomorrow. I hope you have a list of other things that need tending, else it's going to look mighty suspicious my being out there with a hoe when there's snow on the ground."

"I gave you a list earlier."

He shrugged. "Can't remember half of what you said."

She huffed. "I'll write it down tonight."

His eyes twinkled. "Good. Now let's go eat. It smells like fried chicken."

❧

If he'd hoped to bring some humor back to the conversation, he failed abysmally. It had been the mention of Martin that had sparked the remoteness in her. He must remember that she was a grieving widow, touched by the war in a way that could never be recompensed.

Though she had mentioned the need to finish up, she remained stock still, her eyes on some distant point that would remain forever a blur to him unless he asked.

He wondered what she would do if he went to his satchel and removed all the things Martin had given to him. How his death must be shattering her. Every day a new crack and another chunk of her spirit broke off, never to be restored. She would hold the things he gave her as precious and dear. . .as she should.

His mind calculated the number of steps it would take for him to reach his pack and retrieve his secrets to share with her. He swallowed. Perhaps it was time. "Ellie."

Her gaze flickered to him, waiting, expectant.

The longing to take the shadows from those eyes pinched at him. He pressed his lips together and held up a finger to indicate that she should give him a minute. But as Theo crossed to his small bag and knelt before it, he realized the danger this revelation would bring to him. Should she demand answers from the Union army, they would in turn want to know where and by whom she had acquired the information.

From a deserter.

A Southern deserter.

His hand closed over the packet of letters.

Behind him, he heard Ellie gasp. He turned as he rose to his feet, surprised to see her disappearing around the corner. "I'm here, Rose."

Theo half turned and toed his sack behind a barrel of potatoes. He reviewed what he could say to account for his presence in the cellar with a grieving widow woman.

Ellie darted back into the room, cheeks flushed. "I think Rose's labor has begun. I'm going to check. You stay here and finish the cleaning."

nine

Ellie found Rose in the middle of the porch, face ashen, her hand pressed against her protruding stomach.

"It woke me up."

Ellie nodded. "How long have you had pain?"

"I was frying chicken and thought it was because I'd been on my feet for too long. I lay down and must have fallen asleep."

She wheeled her friend around as gently as possible and guided her into the house. "Let's get you settled, and I'll go fetch the doctor."

"Send your man," Rose squeezed out before she stopped on their way up the step and sank against the wall.

"I've got to go ask him," Ellie responded when she felt the tension leaving Rose's body.

The pain passed and Rose straightened. "I want to lie down."

Ellie did her best to get as much ready for the impending birth as she could. She set a kettle of water to boil and tried to get Rose to sip tea, but her friend refused it, and when she stiffened up to ride the crest of another pain, Ellie held her hand and prayed for strength. Whether for herself or for Rose, she couldn't be certain.

When Rose relaxed again, Ellie rose. "Let me go ask Theo to fetch Martha." She could sure use her help right now. She hurried down the stairs, out the door, and across the side yard to the cellar door. It took a moment for her eyes to adjust to the dimness of the cellar. "Theo?"

He sat cross-legged, with his back to her, his head raising at her voice. "How is Rose?"

"Holding her own." She studied him. A small book lay open

on his lap, the lantern turned up beside him. "Could you fetch someone from the doctor's office on the corner? Tell them I sent you."

Theo nodded and followed her up the steps. She turned to him as he lowered the cellar doors. In the waning light of day, his eyes were a pale silver. "Please don't forget your accent. And your limp."

***

Theo stared into Ellie's face and wondered if he would have to scrub himself clean of everything remotely Southern in order to survive up here. But it was unfair of him to feel so aggrieved at the thought. It had not been Ellie's idea that he should come north, nor Martin's. He had done so because of his mounting anger over the conditions war imposed, then the desire that the truth be known—an irony now that he realized how much he risked by being in enemy territory.

As Ellie went around the house to go inside, he went through the front gate to the street and toward the corner building that, upon nearing, clearly showed the sign for a Dr. Selingrove. No doubt the man would be elderly, what with most of the younger men fighting the war.

Theo opened the door, a slow heat taking the chill from his skin. The office seemed still, as if frozen in time. Dust tickled his nose. Instruments gleamed behind the glass of a locked cabinet with a gleaming glass front. A small desk in the corner of the room seemed too neat for that of a busy doctor's office.

A light shuffle alerted him, and Theo turned, rehearsing Ellie's list—limp and talk like a Yankee. Footsteps indicated someone's approach. Something strange accompanied the sounds of the steps, a rustling, but before his mind could process the sound, the person appeared.

Bright, dark eyes stared at him with a cool reserve and a proud tilt to the head. An unmistakable, though silent, challenge.

Whatever Theo expected, it had not been this. He felt raked

by the piercing dark eyes of the black woman. "I'm looking for Dr. Selingrove."

"He's not here. It's just me."

Theo's mind stumbled over that. Hadn't Ellie said to come here, to the doctor's office on the corner? "You mean, he's out on a call?"

The woman's direct gaze didn't waver. "No."

He chafed at the delay. "I was told to fetch the doctor."

The woman's chin inclined another inch. "You sent by Miss Ellie?" But the question apparently didn't require an answer because she was already moving, picking up a black bag that rested in the vacant chair behind the desk.

He flinched as the realization pricked that the woman was intent upon leaving with him to help Rose. "I was told to fetch the doctor," he parroted his earlier statement, unable to process this black woman's role in a doctor's office. Or at least, what she supposed her role to be.

As the woman bore down on him, he held up his hand, palm out.

She stopped, her eyes no more downcast than a white man's.

Not something Theo was used to seeing, though he knew the Northern blacks had far superior opinions of themselves. "We'll wait for Dr. Selingrove."

He thought he detected a sparkle in her eyes, but her words were without humor. "You awful young to be waiting on the doctor."

The words didn't make sense to him. Was it her attempt at humor? "How long before he'll be back?"

"Mighty long time."

Theo didn't know what to do. Ellie wanted the doctor, yet this woman seemed determined not to produce more than the merest of replies, and she certainly didn't seem inclined to fetch the man he sought. "Could you send him when he returns?"

Her nod was stiff, almost imperceptible, but he took it as her promise to fulfill his request. He had little choice but to return to Ellie with the disappointing news and the nervous unease that in the absence of a doctor he might somehow be called upon to help.

His return trip to Ellie's home seemed interminable. When he knocked on the front door, he immediately realized the futility of the effort. Ellie would be with Rose upstairs. He let himself into the house, expecting to hear an earth-rending scream from upstairs.

The kitchen seemed serene. Towels folded into a neat stack upon the smooth wood of the kitchen table. Water simmered in a pot on the back of the stove, and a low fire worked its magic to take the chill off the room.

Silence stretched long and worked to soothe Theo's frayed nerves as he sat at the table, unable to conceive what he could do to help, let alone whether he should leave or stay put. His debate over ferreting out Ellie's advice on another doctor or letting her approach him when Dr. Selingrove did not appear upstairs left him befuddled. He did nothing.

When an hour rolled by, he began to pace, saved from wearing a path in the wood floor only by the hollow taps on the stairs that indicated Ellie's patience with the doctor's absence must be thin.

Theo waited for her appearance, nerves stretched taut. His first glimpse of her rooted him to the spot.

She smiled his direction and lifted the stack of towels, eyes shining more than he thought acceptable for a woman facing an impending birth with no help. "Thank you for fetching Martha for us. Rose is doing quite well."

ten

Ellie made as if to turn then realized Theo looked at her with slack-jawed wonder. Fear shot through her as she wondered if he was having a bout with some strange illness.

"Dr. Selingrove is here?"

Ellie lowered the stack of towels to the table. "Why no, of course not. We don't know where Robert is, to be truthful."

"Robert?"

Ellie shifted her weight, frustrated at the delay explaining would force. "Robert Selingrove is Rose's husband. He joined the Northern army some time ago. It's been months since Rose has heard from him, and he's believed to be missing in action, dead, or a prisoner."

"Then who is up there? With Rose?"

"You mean Martha?"

"Martha?"

She nodded. "She's Robert's midwife, but she knows more than most doctors."

"But she—I mean, how. . ."

A muffled scream rent the air.

Ellie clutched the towels tighter to her chest and spun on her heel, heart slamming against her ribs. It was hard enough for Rose to endure the unknown of Robert's whereabouts, but to have his child with that knowledge. . . Her throat closed over that grief.

੨੦

Theodore could endure no more. The muted moans and occasional cries jangled his nerves and sent him fleeing from the kitchen and to the sanctity of the cellar. Chills held him captive as he dropped to the floor.

In his ears he heard not the moans of a woman in labor but of his comrades, his friends, shot full of shrapnel, falling to the ground and writhing in pain. The spot vacated by his fallen friend was replaced by another familiar face and together they advanced. In his head, the cacophony of war set his skull to throbbing. He heard a blast, heard yet another scream, and watched the man beside him go to his knees then fall face forward, hand clutching his midsection, blood streaming through his fingers.

Theodore sucked air into his lungs and tried to block the deluge of painful memories. It seemed the further he got from the war the more the memories plagued him. Was it his own guilty conscience? He had left his friends to warn Ellie out of disgust for the deed and respect and love for his cousin. No matter what, it seemed he was a coward.

Coward. The single word seemed to explode in his mind, and he felt the weight of the label pull at him, demanding penance. Images of fallen comrades, of Martin as he tried to halt his execution, bit at his soul, and he fell into a restless sleep full of blood and screams.

The earth below him seemed to shake, and someone grabbed his arm to pull him forward. He didn't want to advance. Not into the enemy's line, but the hand would not let go.

"Theo!" The voice came close to his ear, pitched low, yet higher in tone. "Theo, wake up."

He could feel the hand tug at him and realized it was not a dream at all. When he opened his eyes, Ellie stared down into his face with watchful eyes and sober concern.

"Settle down. You were screaming so loud I feared you were hurt."

He blinked and relaxed. Her words sunk in slowly as his mind returned to the present. No war. No men surrounding him, running. No shots. Just Ellie and the smells of dirt and overripe apples.

He covered his face with his hands to staunch the sob of relief and cover the emotion that flooded his senses. He shuddered.

"You were dreaming," Ellie stated, her tone sympathetic.

No, he wanted to correct her. Dreams are light things, not terror-riddled images of men so real he could see their faces, hear their voices, and taste their fear.

Her eyes shifted over his face, and her expression softened. The sight of her empathy made him turn his face away. He gasped to staunch the tears then felt something soft press into the palm of his hand. He stared down at her hand nestled in his.

"Martin came home only once. He had nightmares, too." Her voice became a whisper. "It must have been terrible."

He wanted to explain the horror, but words failed him. Instead, he pulled his hand from hers and pushed into a sitting position. "I'm sorry."

Her compassionate expression rolled over him, and he found himself wanting nothing more than to pull her into his embrace and feel the comforting warmth of another human. Someone alive and real and unmarred from the war. Again he forced the urge back. She would not welcome the advance and would never understand the frailty he felt or the security her presence offered.

She tugged on her skirts and rose to her knees, her smile more relaxed. "It's a boy."

The words seemed strange, yet it jarred his mind to a world far from that of his nightmares. Rose. Of course. "A boy?" He forced a smile.

"I thought the cries were from him, but the sounds weren't those of an infant."

He squeezed his eyes shut. "I'm sorry," was all he could think to offer.

The muscles in his neck loosened as the last events of his wakefulness slid into sharp focus. Rose. Dr. Selingrove. The mysterious Martha. He blinked and wondered at the beauty of new life. One untouched by such things as he had known in the war. He forced his mind away from that thought, knowing it would only pull him down.

"You never got supper. You must be starved, and you were right. There's a whole platter of fried chicken upstairs."

He didn't like the way she was looking at him. Maybe he'd smudged something on his face in the midst of his restless sleep, but the thought of food woke his appetite. Perhaps eating would calm him.

"He's the cutest little thing," Ellie said then held out her hand. "Stay here and let me make sure the coast is clear."

His eyes followed her as she disappeared. He could hear the doors opening and her light steps on the wooden planks of the stairs.

He inhaled a slow, long breath, closed his eyes, and rested his head against the wall at his back. A low-level pain pinched at the top of his neck. He shrugged and rolled his head to relieve the tension.

"Come on up," Ellie's voice whispered down to him. As he emerged, she continued her scan of the area. With a flick of her hand, she motioned him forward. "There are some things that need fixing on the house itself, starting with the porch."

A lone horseman trotted up toward the drive and guided the horse toward Ellie's house. Ellie stiffened then relaxed and lifted her voice. "There are some supports on the front porch that need straightening."

Puzzled by her words, he cast her a sidelong glance. She lifted a hand to point to a sagging section of the porch. He caught on to the ploy she was using and played along with his role as a handyman being shown what needed to be done.

"The fence needs a good whitewash, though it might be best to wait on that since cold weather will hit in full force at any time." She waved toward the man dismounting from a black mare, a uniform of blue covering his slender form.

Theo's spine went ramrod straight. In a reflexive action, his hand went for his Colt, but as the man neared, Theo realized the folly of his actions and relaxed. He was not in battle. Far away from the fields that had honed his instinct, not so much to kill the enemy, but for survival.

In the growing dusk, the stranger stroked along his horse's neck and lifted his broad-brimmed hat from his head, revealing wiry gray hair to match his beard.

Beside him, Ellie grew still, her mouth firmed into a hard line.

He didn't like what he was seeing in her expression and wondered if the man's presence meant trouble. "Ellie?"

She turned her gaze on him. "It's all right," came her whispered reply. Ellie took a step toward the newcomer.

Theo remained where he was.

As she drew closer to the man, he turned from his horse and gave her a hug that seemed awkward for both of them. They exchanged words too low for his ears.

Theo stepped forward at Ellie's encouragement. "This is the help I just hired. We were just talking about the work that. . ." Her voice faded.

Horror edged up Theo's spine as his gaze locked with the man. The hair. Those eyes. That beard. He'd seen that profile once before.

Ellie's voice, oblivious to his sudden tension, continued, "I'd like you to meet Theo."

eleven

Theo left her alone with her uncle but returned in time to eat with them. Several times Ellie caught him casting sidelong glances at Uncle Ross. And in turn, when Theo wasn't looking, her uncle's expression would become questioning as he took in the hired man. That Theo knew her uncle was obvious, though she wasn't sure if her uncle merely picked up on Theo's hard stares or if he had seen Theo before but couldn't place him. Other than her wedding, which her uncle didn't attend, she couldn't recollect one time when the two would have met over a family event.

The meal she offered provided more of the same behavior between the two, though Theo kept his head down most of the time and remained quiet unless directly addressed. If she hadn't already invited him for fried chicken, she would have suggested he use the time to settle in the barn and allow her to bring him a plate. She forked a bite of chicken and slipped it into her mouth.

"You're quiet, Ellie. Have you been alone so long that you've forgotten how to be social?"

Though her uncle's comment seemed harmless, and there was a twinkle in his eyes, the chunk of meat she'd been chewing seemed suddenly flavorless and dry. She washed it down with water and pasted on a smile. "There's been a lot going on. Rose had her baby right before you arrived."

"Ah. That would be your neighbor?"

"Her husband hasn't returned from the war, and she hasn't heard from him in months."

"Most unfortunate. What regiment?"

"The 28th Pennsylvania, I believe. As surgeon."

"Generals Lee and McClellan agreed to grant surgeons neutral status, so even if captured by the Southerners, they wouldn't be imprisoned."

"That's a comfort."

There was a long pause in which Ellie struggled to find something civil to say to her uncle. She knew all too well that his visit wasn't a simple social call. "I expect you came here seeking my answer to your proposition."

Her uncle made good use of his napkin then shoved his nearly empty plate back. "You're as forthright as ever, Ellie, my dear. Yes, I wondered why I never received an answer. But then mail service isn't always reliable. I was in the area." He paused and seemed to collect his thoughts. "You must agree, Ellie, that your newfound widowhood would be much less taxing if you allowed me to help."

She cast a glance at Theo. He caught her eye and pushed back from the table. "I'd better turn in for the night."

"You're not going to stay for Rose's pie?"

"I expect you two have business to discuss," he said in a perfect Yankee accent. "I wouldn't want to hinder."

Ellie stood up, tense at the thought of his leaving her with her uncle. "At least stay for pie."

His presence offered her a modicum of protection against what would certainly be her uncle's long diatribe on the reasons why a woman should not be hindered by "business." Since Martin's death she'd received several letters from her uncle Ross inquiring if he could help.

She didn't know if it was her tone or Theo's hunger or simply an act of kindness on his part, but he nodded and lowered himself back down onto the chair.

As she crossed the room to slice the pie, Uncle Ross wasted no time in peppering Theo with questions about his heritage and upbringing. Subjects that had her holding her breath and straining for his answers. She sliced two large pieces and a smaller one for herself.

Theo's answers were vague. He'd grown up in the North. Happy childhood. Normal boyish pranks. No lies in anything he'd revealed so far, but she wondered if her uncle would ask the ultimate question. "Why aren't you fighting?"

She hurried to get the plates to the table and plunked one down in front of Uncle Ross before further questions could slip from his mouth. He frowned up at her then down at the plate. How was it her once lighthearted, fun-loving uncle had become such an uptight old man since her mother's death? Whatever the reason, she didn't like the change.

He lifted his fork and dug in. "Your mother's pies were unbeatable. I still remember her making me a cherry pie when she was sixteen."

Ellie set the other wedge in front of Theo. "It's apple."

Theo nodded and clipped off a small wedge of pie with the edge of his fork.

"Reminds me of the old days," Uncle Ross said, his lips smacking. He shoved another generous bite into his mouth. His head bobbed in rhythm to his chewing. "Really good, Ellie."

"Thank you." She caught Theo's glance and nodded, hoping he might understand the words to mean far more than a trite answer to her uncle's appreciation for pie.

As soon as she sat across from her uncle, he crammed the last bite into his mouth and shoved his plate away.

Her mind shuffled for something to say to distract him from further questions of Theo, and she decided to take the offensive. "I received your latest letter earlier today, so you can imagine how surprised I am at this visit."

"You haven't answered any—"

Ellie held up her hand. "I didn't answer, Uncle, because the answer has not changed. I am not selling the farm. There are too many memories, and it was my mother's legacy to me."

Uncle Ross's nostrils flared, and his eyes narrowed. "Don't you think it might be too much for you to handle, my dear? You could sell it to me at a good profit and leave all the fuss of renting it out and the lands—"

"No." The word slipped out on a rising wave of frustration. She popped a bite of pie into her mouth to buy her time to think.

A storm rose in her uncle's dark eyes. He glanced over at Theo then back at her. She could see that he wondered about the relationship between them.

In an effort to cut off the inquiry sure to come, she turned to Theo. "Before you leave this evening, we need to make a list of the things you'll be working on in addition to what we've already discussed."

Theo inclined his head. "A sound idea, Mrs. Lester."

"I'll be staying the night, Ellie. I assume the guest room is available? I'd like to turn in early."

She would not rise to the bait he laid, chagrined at the suggestion behind his question. "The linens are fresh, though the room may be a bit dusty from disuse."

There, let him chew on that for a while. But if she hoped to dissuade her uncle from further debate on any subject, he disappointed her.

"We'll speak more of this tomorrow. I'd like to look the property over if you don't mind. For old times' sake, you understand."

twelve

"My foot."

Theo suppressed the chuckle that threatened to erupt as Ellie's words, spoken in a whisper after her uncle left the room, showed exactly what she thought of the older man's idea.

"What farm is he speaking of?"

Ellie met his gaze. "Ever since Martin's death was made public knowledge, he has wanted to buy the farm Mother left to me."

"A farm?" He cocked his head, absorbing the fact she had just shared and what it meant in relation to what he had witnessed. "If it's yours, why do you live here?"

Ellie lowered her eyes. "She left me this house as well."

So Ellie Lester was a rich woman. If Uncle Ross was the man Theo thought him to be. . . Theo rubbed a finger over the bridge of his nose and scratched down the growing stubble along his jaw. He had no proof. There were hundreds of thousands of bearded men fighting in the war. The sight of Ross's beard and general physique seemed similar, but his position wasn't such that he could easily point a finger at any man, Union or Confederate.

"Are you not feeling well?"

He clenched his teeth for a second. "I'm fine."

"You should get settled in the stable. At least the air there might be better than. . ." She gave him a huge smile and laughed. He caught on to the turn of her thoughts.

"Fresher?" he suggested.

"Well, maybe not that."

They laughed, their gazes locking. Theo enjoyed the sound

of her laughter and the way her curls brushed against her shoulders with the tilt of her head. What they shared felt a little bit like camaraderie, and the warmth of the emotion bit hard into his soul. He was here to deliver a message—to let a grieving widow know that her husband's death had been anything but accidental, that he was not a casualty of war. Yet here he sat, beguiled by her laughter in a way that was not what he had expected.

She blinked and the fringe of her lashes shadowed her cheek for a slow second. She looked away. "I need to check on Rose. I'll probably stay the night with her."

He rose when she did, watching as she quietly gathered a shawl from a peg on the wall and slipped open the back door.

He followed her onto the back porch. The yard was dark, though the moon shimmied along a gossamer cloud, trying to shine its light. "I'll stay until you're inside."

She turned toward him. "There's no need. Really."

Theo looked out over the yard toward the garden.

Beside him he heard Ellie give a gasp.

He jerked to face her. "What is it?"

Her eyes flicked to his face. "I thought I saw something. Probably a rabbit."

He didn't believe her. The way she hugged herself, her direct gaze seemed forced, as if her eyes wanted to look elsewhere. But she didn't give him time to press her. She shrugged around him and hastened to Rose's back door, giving him a little wave and shutting the door firmly.

Theo scanned the yard, seeing nothing out of the ordinary. Frustrated by Ellie's swift departure, he whipped around, restless at the idea of retreating to the barn so early. With no choice, he crossed to the stable, glad he'd brought his knapsack and the lantern up from the cellar after Ellie's uncle's arrival.

He touched a match to the wick and allowed the flame to catch before lowering the chimney. Between the straw and the old, dry barn boards, he would have to be careful with the lantern or the whole place would go up in flames. He searched through the tools for a nail, found a hammer, and pounded the spike into a solid support post then hung the lantern from it.

He tugged around a few bales of hay and stacked them to form a low wall. One swipe of a rather dull-edged knife on the tool bench and the strings of another bale broke. He spread the hay around, pushing it into a thick mound for use as a mattress. Then, with nothing else to do, he stretched out and tucked his arms beneath his head.

A dark spot on the beamed ceiling tugged a grimace from him. Evidence of a leaky spot. Right above his head. With a grunt he got to his feet and studied the ceiling. Only the place where he had been lying showed signs of previous leaks, so he swept his pile of hay to the other side of his little space. Satisfied he had thwarted being watered like a tree should it rain, he stretched out again and closed his eyes.

Within seconds he sat up, nerves stretched taut. It worried him that he would have another bad dream. He didn't want to remember. He did his best to focus on the things around him, the tools and what he planned to accomplish the next day, but his mind stumbled when he thought of Ellie. How she might look holding the new baby. The straggle of cobwebs clinging to her blond hair when she'd been cleaning the cellar. Her long lashes and flashing blue eyes. . .

Theo reached out and pulled his knapsack closer. He needed a distraction, but thinking of Ellie only churned emotions he thought best left alone. She was a widow, and he was a deserter with nothing to offer. He dug around a bit and extracted the small Bible he carried. Its cool leather and the familiar cracks in the cover brought a measure of comfort. And he needed comfort.

❧

Ellie held the baby close as Rose made herself comfortable in bed. "Thank you, Ellie. I can take him now."

"Have you thought of a name?"

Rose's features pinched. "Colin was Robert's choice. Colin Daniel."

Ellie wrapped the blanket more snugly and placed the child into his mother's arms. "A strong name for a strong boy." She straightened, trying to hide her anxiousness to be outside again.

She hated outright lying to Theo, but the sight of the open gate, coupled with the face of her normal contact person, a black man named Saul, had so startled her that she knew the black man was showing himself for only one reason. And it was important. His very presence communicated that she should be on the alert, even if his overalls and the casual way he stood against the open gate said nothing more than a man out for a late evening stroll to others.

"If there's nothing else you need right now, I'll go back and fetch a plate for you. Food will help you get your strength back."

Rose made a face and adjusted the baby's position.

"Martha told me to make you eat something. She worries that you're too thin."

Rose sighed. "If I must."

Relieved to have an excuse to leave, she paced her steps so her footfalls wouldn't seem rushed to Rose's ears. Rose's needs had taken over an hour to tend to. She wondered what Saul's message might be. . .and dreaded finding out.

The first thing Ellie noted upon being outside was the light flickering from the stable onto a patch of grass only a few feet away from the still-open gate. She'd never realized how dangerous Theo's presence would be to her and the contacts that helped her get runaways to safety. That he knew about her dealings in the Underground Railroad did little to quell her fears. He was a Southerner, after all.

She saw no sign of Saul now and didn't expect to. Staying risked people getting suspicious of his lingering presence at the gate.

Ellie moved into the circle of light bleeding from the barn window onto the brown grass where her backyard joined with that of her neighbor's. Her stomach heaved with dread. With a deep breath to steady her nerves, she moved closer to the garden gate.

From there she could see the worn path that snaked behind the next three houses and down to the offices of Dr. Selingrove, Rose's husband. It was the same path Saul would have taken earlier.

She skimmed over her neighbor's garden to her left, a dark, eerie place of twisted trees and gnarled old roses, then to the stand of evergreens to the right of the path.

Something moved among the evergreens. She blinked, unable to penetrate the darkness or make out the form of anyone. Maybe it was a dog. Still, her stomach clenched in fear. What if it was a trap? A stranger sniffing around for his runaway slaves who had discovered her part in the operation.

She shivered. In that moment of uncertainty, she retreated a few steps closer to where the light from the lantern offered her some security. For surely if she cried out, Theo would come to her rescue.

"Miss Lester?" The whisper caught Ellie's attention, and the form of the slender black midwife emerged from the path, her black bag gripped in her hand.

Ellie bit back a response. The woman had left Rose only two hours previous. She would not return unless asked, which meant. . .

"I'm glad you came." Ellie nodded and swung the gate shut behind Martha.

Martha said nothing but followed Ellie into Rose's kitchen. When she turned, Martha sat at the table, her black gaze hard on her. "He came to me."

Saul.

Of course. Ellie turned the logic of it over in her mind. He must have heard about Rose's delivery and known Martha would be a logical choice to deliver his news.

"There is a husband and wife who could not move. The woman is ill and expecting. I done what I could for her, but they needin' a place to go for the night 'fore they move on."

It would be risky to direct the woman and her husband to the cellar with Uncle Ross's room not far above. Ellie shook her head. "I can't do anything with my uncle here."

"If she gives birth, she will need to be far away. You have a farm?"

The farm! Her mind tripped over possibilities. Her renters stayed in the main house and had a garden on the acre directly surrounding, but the springhouse, barn, and summer kitchen were all possibilities. "I can't take them tonight."

Martha gave a slight nod.

Ellie didn't want to ask where they would stay that night. A pregnant woman ready to give birth would be a huge risk factor. "When I'm ready for them at the farm, I'll show our signal and expect them after dark."

"I hoping to get them to Philadelphia as soon as possible. Pray for an easy birth."

She led the way up the steps to Rose's room where the young mother was just finishing nursing her son. "Martha came to check on you," Ellie said quietly, running a finger over the baby's head.

Rose lifted an eyebrow. "Really?"

"You make good and sure the mother gets her rest and is eating as she should."

Rose gave Ellie a sheepish look. "I guess Ellie has been telling on me, but I was going to eat."

Ellie just smiled.

Martha turned to her, a slight twinkle in her eyes. "You get some food."

"I feel fine, Martha." She stared down at the bundle in her arms. "But I worry about. . ."

Ellie left them alone, her mind already considering and rejecting a hundred scenarios on how to transport the slaves such a distance without being seen. She put together a tray of toast and peach preserves for Rose and delivered it to the room. Martha, she had no doubt, would make sure the young mother ate.

She went back to worrying over the problem of transporting the slaves without being seen. And the frequency of the trips might lead someone to grow suspicious. And how would she care for the runaways when they were so far away? She couldn't leave Rose.

The solution presented itself as she stepped onto the back porch and laid eyes on the light still glowing from the stable.

thirteen

Theo had been startled at the sound of Ellie's voice asking if she could talk to him, but, his eyes weary from reading and his mind still unable to sleep, he had welcomed the company. She scooted around the bales of hay and sat down at his invitation. He sat across from her, noting her grave expression. "Horses aren't much company." He tilted his head to indicate the bay mare and the gray. "A one-sided conversation isn't very appealing."

Her face lost some of the tightness and a small smile curved her lips. "No, I don't expect Libby and Mina are much company." She twisted on the bale to stroke the nose of the mare who hung her head over the stable door to get attention.

For the long minute she petted the horse, he admired her silhouette—the curve of light along her cheekbones and the slender hands that moved from the horse's muzzle to her ears. Her beauty stirred in him a hunger for companionship. Human contact. Home-cooked meals and fresh linens. A cozy fireplace and the soft touch of Ellie's lips on his at the end of a long day working. . . .

He shook himself and straightened, realizing his image had been that of Ellie as his wife, not as that of a widow grieving for her husband. What would Martin say if he knew Theo's thoughts had stirred in the direction of becoming his replacement in Ellie's life? The idea held him suspended in horror for a moment, until it occurred to him that Martin would be pleased.

Ellie's hands fell to her sides and she sighed, turning to face him. "I came to both ask a favor and offer a solution."

He shook the thoughts from his head. "I'm listening."

"I don't know how long Uncle Ross will be staying, and I know it's not comfortable for you in the cellar, or even in here. You see. . ." She clasped her hands together and bit her lip.

He wasn't sure where she was headed with it all and decided to remain quiet.

"I thought it might be nice for you to have a place over at our family farm. All to yourself. For however long you want or need to stay. But there will be certain responsibilities." She wiped her hands on her skirts.

He sensed her frustration and waited patiently for her to continue.

She met his gaze for a second before glancing away then released a sigh. "I'll just come out and say it. You know what I'm doing, and I know what you are. I need your secrecy just as much as you need mine. Hanging around here posing as my handyman is a good idea, but it puts you at risk as well. At the farm you'll be away from curious eyes. But I need help." Her blue eyes on him were imploring. "I have a young couple. The woman is pregnant, due to give birth any day, and I need a way to get them out to the farm. I was thinking of the wagon. Maybe you could put in a false bottom? I've heard of others using that method to transport—" She shrugged. "You know what I mean."

He scanned the stable, his gaze landing on the wagon itself. "I would need wood and tools."

"There are repairs that need to be done on the buildings at the farm. I had some repairs made to the farmhouse before the renters moved in, so you don't need to disturb them. But there is plenty of other work to keep you busy. There's a lot of old wood there. You could take Libby over before sunrise with the wagon, and as long as you're done with the false bottom by evening tomorrow—"

"Evening?"

"That's when we're going to make the transfer. If Uncle is here and demands to go out with us again, for whatever reason, at least he won't see the people. And it'll put distance between you and him."

He stroked his hand down his face, wanting to ask for a razor.

"Would you like to shave?"

The way she read his thoughts. . . . Her need to put distance between her uncle and him made him suspect his covert glances at Ross had not gone undetected. He would have to be more careful to guard his expressions.

"Do you know my uncle?"

There it was. The question he had asked himself a hundred times. "I thought I did, but there are so many gray-headed men with beards. . . ."

She seemed content with his answer. She leaned forward, expression tense. "You'll help me then?"

Theo saw hope flicker in her eyes. Just her asking him to engage in the transfer of slaves was a risk. She had no way of knowing he wouldn't turn her in or take the slaves himself and return them to the South. Other than the fact that she knew his secret as well.

What beckoned him to say yes the most was the prospect of that farm. No cramped cellar. No pitch blackness. Even less chance of being caught. He could go back and forth to her house to make the repairs she had asked to be done there or to help with the garden. He'd be free to move around at whim.

It struck him then that his plans were stretching toward long term. Theo swallowed hard over the constriction in his throat. What kept him here? Why didn't he just tell Ellie the terrible news and all that he suspected, give her the letters, and leave?

❧

Ellie hung suspended, breathless, waiting for Theo to answer the simple question. She knew he must be guessing how desperate she was to ask him, what with all he would risk helping her. What she didn't prepare herself for was the intensity of his stare. She felt pinned by that pewter gaze, as if he was searching for a hidden motive. A vulnerability she hadn't expected to see. Did he really think she would lure him to help her then turn him in? "You know I won't betray you, Theo. I could never do that."

Something shifted in his expression, heightened.

She tried to draw a breath, confused at her inability to move beneath that commanding stare. "You're. . .you're Martin's favorite cousin."

He inhaled sharply and scratched his jaw, turning away. "Yes. Of course. Tomorrow evening will work fine."

He stood and she did the same. She'd never seen this side of him. Stealthy. Curious. Fearful. Again, his gaze searched her face, until he shouldered his way past her and out into the night, leaving her to contemplate the rear end of the dappled gray. Why were men so complicated? Correction. Man, not men.

Martin she had understood all too well. From the time they started courting he had been easygoing and kind, though quiet. She had loved to hear his laughter. But this man confused her. He garbled her senses and made her wonder what it would be like to have a husband again. To love and be loved.

Guilt washed over her. How could she forget so easily all that she'd lost on that battlefield? So much more than a husband, but a companion and friend, a way of life. Theo was only Martin's cousin, and though he must surely struggle with being forced to trust the enemy—her—didn't he realize she was making the same sacrifice by asking for his help?

Libby swished her tail and broke the reverie of Ellie's thoughts. At one time she might have prayed for guidance, but God had seemed far away since Martin's death. What she needed was sleep. With her uncle Ross so close, she knew taking care of Rose, sparring with Uncle Ross, and the "cargo" left in her care would tax her more than normal.

She swept open the door of the stable and stepped into the night. She waited a moment, allowing her eyes to adjust to the dimness, and swept the yard for signs that Theo might be nearby. Still puzzled over his reaction yet buoyed by his commitment to help, she crossed the yard. Maybe all he needed was a good night's sleep, too.

She was about to close the door behind her when his voice came to her. "Good night, Ellie."

Startled, she scanned the yard, still unable to pinpoint his location. "Good night," she whispered, unsure if he would even hear her reply.

fourteen

Theo had watched from the shadow of the tree as Ellie closed the door after his "Good night." When he saw a light flicker upstairs, he finally pushed away from the trunk and wandered back to the barn. He bedded down, hoping sleep would claim him quickly, before he had to rise for his predawn escape to the farm. But he lay there, unable to get the images of Ellie out of his mind.

He pulled into a sitting position, draping one arm across a bent knee, and lowered his head to work kinks out of the muscles in his shoulders. He forced himself to think beyond the stable and the farm and the runaway slaves he would be working to help. He would help Ellie out, give her the letters, and leave. West would probably be a good direction to follow, and the thought of owning a ranch, or even working as a ranch hand, appealed to him.

What he couldn't allow was the feelings Ellie stirred. Just sitting across from her in the barn, their knees inches apart, her blue gaze running the gamut of emotions. Seeing her profile and aching to touch her cheek or hold her hand had gnawed at him. Then, as she was asking him about her uncle and if he would help, he had been certain he could trust her. He had even given consideration to the rising thought that she might be able to love him back, but when she had implied she would keep his secret, not out of any emotion for him but because he was Martin's cousin, he'd felt like she'd punched him in the gut.

It would do him well to remember the reason he was here. Not to fall in love, but to tell her about Martin and deliver the letters. If he didn't make his escape soon, he might fall in love with her, and that would make leaving impossible. But he couldn't let that happen. Ellie was a woman who deserved a man with something to offer, not a Rebel deserter on the run and in fear, doing odd jobs to make a little money.

He vowed to make the repairs as quickly as possible and get out of there. It was the only solution.

᠅

Uncle Ross's note both perplexed and relieved Ellie. That he had "early morning business to attend to" meant she would be free to help Rose and even make a trip to the farm to check on Theo's progress. His "won't be home until very late" was also something to be cherished. Still, why come visit her only to go off for an entire day? Maybe he was hoping she would soften in his absence. And with his return sometime "very late" she worried he might get back just as they prepared to load the couple.

She went straight over to Rose's house and scrambled an egg for her friend, poached one for herself, and took the toast from the top of the cookstove.

Rose blinked her eyes open, and Ellie saw right away the signs that her friend got little sleep. In the swirl of last-minute plans, she'd forgotten her promise to stay with Rose.

"I must look a sight. I couldn't relax then thought I would roll on him." She gave a sigh. "It was a terrible night."

"I should have stayed. I'm sorry." Ellie waited for Rose to maneuver herself up in bed before she placed the tray in front of her friend and slid the plate onto the surface. "I'll hold pumpkin."

Rose laughed. "I didn't think I would be hungry, but I am." She winced. "Sore, too."

Ellie bent to pull the bundled babe close to her. "Baby Colin," she breathed the name in awe. "He's so perfect."

"A miracle."

A quiver in Rose's voice made Ellie raise her head. Her friend's eyes were squeezed shut, and her face flushed from the effort to hold her tears at bay. She scooted onto the bed beside the woman and put her free arm around her shoulders. Rose immediately broke down, her sobs tearing from her chest, wringing tears from Ellie as well.

Through the entire ordeal Rose had been brave and hopeful that her husband would return. In Ellie's darkest hour, her friend had been there for her, offering a shoulder to cry on and doing kind deeds. Together they had fought their own war, and Rose's war still raged.

Ellie wiped her tears and pulled the baby closer as he began to squirm, no doubt troubled by all the noise. His face reddened.

When his mewing began in earnest, Rose sniffed one last time and reached for him.

Ellie stroked her hair back as her friend nuzzled the baby's cheek and encouraged him to nurse. "You really must eat something," she encouraged.

"I will. I promise." Rose raised her swollen eyes to Ellie. "You've been such a comfort to me, Ellie."

"We have been to each other."

"Yes, God does know what we need in the midst of sorrow."

"You have hope that as a doctor Robert will be safe. And now you have baby Colin to bring you comfort." Her throat closed. The unspoken lay between. Ellie's lip quivered, and she bit it and pushed to her feet. "I've got other things to tend to. Uncle Ross isn't home until late tonight and there's laundry to be done and an afternoon meal to be cooked."

"And God to run away from."

She spun toward Rose. "That's not fair!"

Her friend's gaze held a distinct challenge. "Isn't it?"

"You haven't lost your husband. How could you understand?"

"Why does a departure from God need to be understood?

It is what it is, Ellie. Nothing should separate you from God. He's the comfort you lack now. Isn't that what you were just saying? I have hope Robert will return and now I have little Colin, and you have nothing?"

Ellie pressed her knees against the edge of the mattress and bowed her head. She should have known Rose would see through her.

"You think I don't see your frustration over what you perceive to be God taking Martin from you?"

"I don't feel that way." Yet she could not deny the evidence. She'd laid down excuse after excuse for avoiding any form of church function, and her Bible, once sampled from daily with great delight, lay on a shelf in her room, coated with dust. She squeezed her eyes shut. "It's so hard."

The bed creaked and sheets rustled. She felt Rose's arms stretch around her waist and her head nestle against her back. "Would Martin want this for you?"

"How do I know what he would want? He's not here."

"You would know in your heart."

Her heart. It had become a cold, hard thing. Frozen by the absence of love promised to her in vows breathed by a smiling Martin on their wedding day. It all seemed such a long-ago dream.

Though she had managed to get through the hot summer days by concentrating on the garden and helping Rose put up vegetables, the hollow nights of winter nipped at her heels. Work would be centered around tasks that could be done inside where the walls echoed the roar of silence. She knew it waited for her, just as it did in the long, restless nights before sleep gave her relief.

"Ellie, why don't you talk to someone? The pastor's wife?"

"Because all it does is stir the thoughts of forever without him."

Rose squeezed her hand. "I know there's no words that will

take away your pain. But there is a promise in the Bible. . ."

Fragments of scripture after scripture flitted through Ellie's mind. She could think of many that offered hope and encouragement, but nothing seemed able to penetrate the deep, dark spot where death had suffocated her joy.

"God promises that time will heal our hurts, Ellie." Rose tugged on her hand until Ellie met her gaze. "Do you believe that? *Can* you believe that?"

She didn't have an answer. Oh, she wanted to believe, to feel the security she once felt and believe that even this, the death of her husband, could be for her good. But even the thought of it seemed incongruous.

Still, Rose wanted an answer. Expected it. "I'll try. That's all—" Her voice broke, and she pressed a hand to her lips.

She rushed from the room, stopping on the landing and pushing her fists into her eyes to staunch tears. *I don't know how to heal. How to believe through this that You still love me. . .*

fifteen

In the swelling light of the rising sun, a haze of rainbow hue colored the underbelly of the low clouds. Theo shivered in the cold and huddled deeper into the flannel shirt. With the wagon safely out of sight and the horse contentedly munching oats, he surveyed the expanse of farmland stretching before him. He had passed the farmhouse a quarter mile down the road, well hidden from the barn tucked behind a tall privet hedge, assuring him privacy, and the slaves as well when they made their journey to the springhouse later that night.

It had been a walk down memory lane for him. He clearly remembered the wedding in the backyard of the farmhouse, then the laughter and quiet stealth required of him and his other cousins hiking the bridal bed to the ceiling. Such good memories gave him confidence, even if the damage done by the Battle of Gettysburg to the structures dimmed the reality somewhat. The work would be good for him.

He began by inspecting the wagon then the boards stuffed into a corner of the barn. Building the false bottom would not take as long as he had first thought. Since the wagon bed was solid, he need only place a strip of wood around the perimeter of the sides then secure boards together and lay them on top. As Ellie suggested, the barn held all types of tools to get the job done.

He stroked his chin, clean shaven now, the razor waiting for him just inside the barn door when he woke. She'd left it for him without a sound. Perhaps he slept and she didn't wish to wake him.

He raised his face to the meager warmth the morning sun

provided, its feeble heat welcome on the smooth skin of his jaw. He recalled a similar morning, surrounded by his comrades, hot sun beating down on them. Those happy times that knit together a group of men who otherwise would have never known each other. Chad's smiling face and bright red hair. Tom's limp, a result of a still-healing ankle. Bud's solemn eyes and tense smile, his expression the embodiment of everyone's fears for the next day, the next battle.

The vision shifted and Theo tried to shut out what he knew would be a darker memory. He pushed up the sleeves on his shirt and began sorting through the pile of boards. In his mind, he heard Bud's voice. His proclamation the night before they would engage in battle at Chancellorsville.

"It's gonna happen."

Theo's hands began to shake. He pushed at the thought and lifted another board, anything to block the stream of memories he had unleashed.

War. Fighting. Blood.

He gulped air, and the board he held fell to the ground.

Bud.

He saw the boy's face in his mind, a tanned face. A Georgia boy who had signed up because he believed war was an adventure. The many skirmishes soon taught Bud otherwise, as it had taught them all. That night Bud had slept fitfully.

Theo's skin crawled, and he sank to the ground, cradling his head, recalling the muffled sound of Bud's tears.

"What's the matter, Bud?" But Theo had already known the boy's fear. He placed his hand on the slim shoulders of the boy-man and shook him gently.

Bud's crying ceased, but he didn't open his eyes.

Theo retreated to his own blanket, pulling it up high to ward off the chill of that May evening as much as to quell nerves stretched taut by Bud's strange dreams and bold proclamations that always seemed to come true.

He had learned to console Bud with his voice. Would often break out into hymns when Bud seemed bothered or anxious, inevitably the night before they took on the enemy.

Hymns.

In the barn, Theo forced himself to stand and raised his voice to full volume to push against the memories. The hymn he remembered best. "Rock of Ages." And as he sang, he picked up the board he had abandoned earlier. He forced out the next verse of the song, feeling the steadiness of his mind returning.

By noon he had installed the lip on which the false bottom would rest and still he sang. Song after song. His voice growing weaker from the strain. When he could sing no longer, he led Libby out to the small pasture and let her loose then returned to the barn where he continued to measure boards and cut them to size.

He stretched his arms above his head and worked his head from side to side. Some sound brought his mind to full alert, and he turned toward the doorway of the barn where he'd left the doors open just wide enough to allow natural light to permeate his work area. A horse buzzed its lips, and Theo's mind tripped over one excuse after another to make plausible to a visitor his presence in a barn that he didn't own.

A hand appeared along the edge of the barn door. "Theo?"

Tension ebbed from him as he recognized Ellie's voice. And not her voice.

"Yeah."

When she pulled the door open a little more and appeared in that opening, sunlight washed her in its bright rays. "I wondered if there was anything you needed." She wore a fresh gown of lemon yellow.

As she neared him, he cleared his throat and added another reason to the list of why he needed to leave. Ellie Lester did not need a man haunted by visions of his past. She needed someone who could shrug off the war instead of allowing it to become a ball and chain to his emotions.

But even as she closed the distance between them, he knew the truth. He had not escaped soon enough. His heart galloped at the sight of her, and his head filled with the sight of a stray strand of her hair dangling against her neck and of her clear skin. And when she got close enough, he smelled a hint of jasmine.

She stopped in front of him, a question in her blue eyes. He felt her gaze skim along his clean-shaven jaw and saw the small smile of approval that belied the telltale signs of redness rimming her eyes.

"You've been crying." It accounted for the strangeness of her voice and the slight puffiness around her eyes.

"You weren't supposed to notice."

He gave her a small smile and lowered his voice. "A gentleman should always take notice of a woman in distress."

Something akin to panic flashed in the blue depths before she lowered her eyes to the dirt floor.

He cleared his throat again, his voice gravelly from his singing. He was scaring her. Even if he was ready to admit what he could no longer deny, she wouldn't understand. He forced his voice to come out strong. "Nothing has gone wrong, has it?" Yet even as he asked the question, he knew the answer. If she had somehow been discovered or a problem had come up, she would have been more anxious, even fearful.

"Everything is fine."

He could deny those words and pry for the truth, but he had no right to do such a thing, unless... "You won't even tell your cousin what's bothering you?"

Her lips settled into a grim line. "Just missing Martin, I suppose. Maybe feeling sorry for myself."

The willingness with which she shared startled him. No coquettish holding out or games meant to wrap a man in knots as big as the hooped skirts the young Southern belles wore. Still, her grief built a wall of restraint in him. She needed time, not a declaration of love. "He was a good man."

Her stiff nod told him she kept her emotions in check. "Why don't I just look over what you've done and get out of your way?" She did not wait for an answer but stepped around him and to the wagon.

He watched as she inspected his work. If he were to make his escape, he needed to seize the moment and tell her everything. Now was the time. Knowing about Martin's death would bring her a measure of comfort. He could reduce her grief by giving his account. But the truth smacked the face of her trust in him. He was a Confederate. And a deserter. And his accusation would be against a captain in the Union she held so dear, and who perhaps was her uncle.

Theodore licked his lips and shifted his weight, his eyes on her as she ran a hand along the rough wood of the wagon. As she stretched an arm to reach inside and touch the lip of wood he had just installed, he swallowed over the dryness in his throat. As her hair fell about her shoulders in riotous curls and her profile revealed not only the puffiness of her eyes but the grace with which she held herself, Theo closed his eyes tight. Here was a woman whose determination to help others without thought of her own safety and reputation was something he could not only admire but a quality in direct contrast to his own inability to perform. The strength with which she endured losing someone she loved, her desire to help *him*, and her devotion to Rose showed a noble spirit he could not hope to match.

He had waited too long to show her the truth. She would suspect his motive now, and rightly so. But not telling her made him more of a coward than he already was, and he risked losing everything. He would be forced to leave and head west.

Ellie returned to him, her soft smile and a light of appreciation in her eyes squeezing his heart. "You're doing a wonderful job. I can see exactly what you're planning and think the stack of lumber in here would make a good cover for..." A line appeared between her brows. "Theo?"

She touched his arm, and the heat of her fingers added to the torture of his guilty secret. Time seemed to slow in that moment when he stared down at her small hand on his forearm. Her eyes grew wide, and he brought his other hand to cover hers. She tried to draw away, and he could see that she didn't understand. But how could she? He steeled himself against weakness and held her gaze.

"There is something I need to tell you, Ellie. Something I should have said the day you found me."

≈

As Theo walked away from her, toward the stall that held Libby, Ellie stilled herself. She could see by the slump of his shoulders and his hesitant steps that he was bothered. What would he have to tell her? Her mind considered and rejected a thousand things, but nothing made sense.

He knelt at the front edge of the stable and dug into the small knapsack she had seen in the cellar. His hand withdrew a packet of white papers then dug down again to withdraw three loose sheets of paper. He folded them with the other stack and rose, his back to her, head down, the tail of his flannel shirt hanging loose from his trousers. "I met Martin."

She heard his words but didn't understand what he meant. Of course he had met Martin before. Many times because Martin...

"Before Chancellorsville. I knew his regiment. We saw each other across the field as they were retreating from us." He turned toward her, and her eyes went to his face, stiff and paler than normal. "We managed to work out a time to meet in an old, abandoned house that was already torn apart from a battle a week before."

"But...how? You're a..."

"There was a widow woman who helped tend the sick on the battlefield. I got a message to her and told her who to deliver it to. She said she would try. I didn't hear anything for a few days until. . ."

She waited, not knowing what to say.

She startled when Theo sank to the dirt floor, as if his knees could no longer hold his weight. He draped his arms over his bent knees and let his head sink down, shielding his face. The packet lay on his lap.

She knelt beside him, afraid to touch him. "Theo? I don't understand. How?" She shook her head, wondering if she was hearing correctly, concerned by Theo's demeanor and what it might mean. "You're scaring me."

When he lifted his head, his expression was wistful. "Don't mean to. It's just. . ." A shudder swept through him. "There was a young boy. His name was Bud. He was always saying something was going to happen to this one or that one. And it always did." He paused and rubbed his cheek. "I could usually calm him down if I sang to him, but the night before nothing seemed to work. He was convinced his time had come and that something would happen to him that day in battle. And it did." His jaw clenched, his eyes fixed on a distant spot. "I found him facedown. I carried him back. 'Twas the widow woman who found me on the edge of the field. Guess I lost my head a little bit. I don't remember much, except her taking me aside later on and pressing something into my hand."

"Martin?"

"Yes. He wanted to meet on the edge of their camp. Said his captain had a fitful temper for anyone caught sneaking around." He paused and straightened one leg.

"What about Bud?"

Theo chuckled, a dry, humorless sound. "I sat next to him through the night. He was dead before daylight."

"So you didn't meet Martin?"

"We fought all that day. At least I think I did. I remembered shooting and moving and hunkering down in a trench. I wondered what it all meant, and then I didn't care anymore."

His voice caught, and she saw the struggle it took for him to retain his composure. Part of her wanted to reach out to him and tell him it was fine to cry. During his one furlough, Martin had spoken of the horrors he'd seen, but she had also sensed a pocket of emotion that remained untapped.

"I wanted out. Thought of nothing else all that night and up to the time I met Martin. I imagined a bullet in my back at any minute as I crept out of camp that night. Kept hoping it would come." He shook his head. "When I met Martin, he was thin, painful thin. He was writing by the light of the moon filtering through a hole in the ceiling and wall. No lights because light meant we'd be detected. We talked for a long time."

Theo lifted his head and stared her straight in the eye. "Seemed I wasn't alone in wanting to desert. Martin said most everyone he knew had thought of it at one time or another. Even him. He even invited me to visit after the war was over. Said no matter if I was a fool Confederate, I'd still be welcome in his home." Theo's smile melted away as quickly as it appeared. "We agreed to meet again the next night, provided we were still engaged. I slipped off from the cabin first, but then I heard something behind me and hunkered down in some bushes. I saw Martin leave the cabin and heard footsteps right at my ear. A man passed by and then. . .I don't know. There was a shot. And somehow I knew it was Martin that shot was meant for. The same man went by me again, and I caught a glimpse of him. I heard a low moan and knew it was Martin. When I went to him, he was already gone, Ellie. I promise you. There was nothing I could have done."

Stunned by what he was implicating, Ellie raised her hands to her face, processing the information over and over. "He was murdered?"

"That's not all. The man I heard, I saw. Just a glimpse, but I—" He put a hand to his brow and massaged the spot between his eyes.

Ellie chafed at the delay in what he was going to say. She opened her mouth to prompt him when he dropped his hand to his lap and met her gaze.

"The man looked a lot like your uncle Ross."

sixteen

Ellie pressed her fingertips to her lips as the tension built in her neck and shoulders.

"I have no proof," she heard Theo's voice. "But when I saw him the other night, my impression was that I'd seen him before."

Uncle Ross? Shoot Martin for no reason? A curl of doubt wound its way through her mind. It had been Uncle Ross who had delivered the news of Martin's death. His letter assured her that he would oversee the burial. Even in her reply, asking that he bring Martin's body back to Gettysburg, Uncle Ross had indicated it could not be done, and she had accepted his word as a certainty. She drew air into her lungs, determined to hear whatever else Theo had to say before drawing a conclusion. "You. . .went to him."

Theo nodded. "As soon as I could. I knew his effects would be sent home to you under normal circumstances, but I feared the man would come back. Or that Martin's body would be overlooked. I didn't know what to do, so I took what I could." His long fingers wrapped around the packet and held them out to her. "Papers. Letters and the one he was working on in the dark when I arrived. There are a few coins and a bit of money from his pockets, but nothing else."

She accepted the papers, hands trembling. Her mind reeled from all she had heard and from the familiarity of the simple script on those three pages that had no envelope. Martin's last words to her.

Theo got to his feet and moved away. She followed his movement with her eyes, knowing he was putting distance between them to give her privacy.

She ran her fingertip over the small stack of papers in her lap, almost afraid to see what Martin had written to her. He had been a well-spoken man, and his letters were full of details about the men rather than their maneuvers and upcoming plans for battle. As it should be. But she'd stopped receiving letters from him about a month before news of his death. She realized she now held those letters. He hadn't stopped writing her but must have been holding the letters until he could post them.

She picked up the three sheets of loosely folded paper and her hands trembled. As she gently unfolded them, her eyes fell on the familiar handwriting, and she once again heard his voice and saw his smile in her mind's eye.

My Dearest Ellie,

How I long to be home again. I am more convinced with each passing day that war is more terror and fear than victory and valor. It will take every day of my life to forget memories etched in my mind. I fear only heaven can take away the horror of this living hell. Your softness of spirit and carefree laughter keep me sane yet bring such a terrible longing for home that I fear I have, more than once, been tempted to leave without regard for punishment.

I hate the pitting of man against man. We are given little to eat and made to walk miles, under the extra weight of our packs. My bones ache with a tiredness I cannot name. Only when I see your smile or hear your laughter does my heart rest from it all, if only briefly.

I hope with the next letter you will send a likeness of yourself, so that your face won't go blurry in my mind's eye. I fear it will. Some days I think it already has and that the woman I perceive is only that of a long-ago memory, an angel who is there but just out of reach.

Tears welled in her eyes and she blinked, releasing them to stream down her cheeks. *Oh, Martin.*

❧

Theodore saw it coming. He had known the letter would stir her grief, but he wasn't prepared for the heart-wrenching whimpers that emanated from her lone figure.

Unable to witness her grief without trying his best to quell it, he went out to the pasture to bring Libby back in. When Ellie didn't react to their movements, Theo knew her world was narrowing to that spot of sorrow that no human could touch. How many times had he himself held a fallen comrade and felt that same isolating grief?

Her whimpers turned to something more. Deeper. As if her soul was shattering. He turned back to the board he had been sawing to fit against the others, but he was unable to block out her need. When he could stand it no longer, he laid the saw aside, bumping the sack of nails. They spilled at his feet, but he ignored them.

In a modicum of strides, he covered the distance separating them. "Ellie." The shivering whimpers were building in volume. He cupped her elbows. "Ellie?"

For the time it took him to exhale, she quieted, her gaze focusing on his face. All the pain in her heart reflected in the stormy blue of her eyes. "He's all gone," she whispered, her voice soft and sad, like a small child whose beloved toy had been smashed to bits. Her eyes closed again, and she began to shake her head.

He felt drawn to her grief. Connected in a way he understood all too well, and not at all. His hands slid up her arms, and he pulled her toward him, tucking her head beneath his chin. Her hands clenched the folds of his shirt, and her tears flowed freely. He cupped the back of her head and rocked her gently within his embrace. Her breath coming in gasps, punctuated by mewls that turned him inside out and left him ragged with hurt.

Gradually her sobs gave way to gasping breaths then sniffles. He stroked her hair and felt her shift, releasing his shirt and running a hand under her nose. When she pulled back, he let her go, and an immediate chill filled the space she had occupied.

To give her time to further collect herself, he leaned to pick up the scattered sheets and envelopes and worked them back into a neat pile. He held them out to her, wishing he could see her face then felt the hand of guilt press against his conscience.

"I should have told you sooner. I. . ." He didn't know what more to say. "Ellie. . ."

She hugged herself and lifted her gaze to his. A wan smile played on her lips. "I need to get back."

"Let me go with you."

Her smile became more brilliant. "That's kind of you, but I need time. To think." She took a step toward the barn door and turned. "I'll expect you whenever you've finished."

"I'll be another couple of hours." What else could he say? As much as he wanted to go after her, to erase the pain, he knew his presence was a reminder of what she no longer had.

But there was one thing he could give her. As he watched her disappear from his line of vision, he fully understood the folly of what he felt and the risk of expressing it now, while she still grieved for Martin.

He crossed to the doorway, the words on his tongue as he watched her mount the dappled gray from a boulder. His throat filled as he watched her leave. The lane was empty, and the evergreens blocked his view of the road. In the silence left by her departure, he breathed out what he had dared not say out loud. "I'm loving you, Ellie."

seventeen

Rose said little as Ellie slid the plate onto the tray in front of her friend. Really, Rose had said little for the hour she'd been working on doing laundry and sprucing up her room.

And it suited Ellie fine. The last thing she wanted or needed was to be forced to carry on a conversation she didn't have a heart for. She moved about in a comfortable haze of spent emotional exhaustion, doing the few tasks she knew needed to be done for Rose and baby Colin, in a rush to get back to her place for the evening.

Martha came by in the late afternoon to check on Rose.

When she came back down to the silent kitchen, Ellie made the statement they used as code. "Do you have to go out of town tonight?"

Martha didn't smile, her sharp eyes acknowledging the secret message. "Got to work spreading my garden after sunset. No babies to deliver tonight."

Ellie nodded and walked with Martha to the door, her tension over the slave transfer ebbed at the black woman's reassuring message. "How is Rose, Martha?"

"She fine if she'll stay put. Most want to get up and jump around right away, but you tell her to stay put." Martha placed her hand on the garden gate and paused. "Any news from Dr. Selingrove?"

Ellie knew how much Rose's husband meant to the black woman. "Not yet."

If Martha felt disappointment, her expression did not show it. She merely gave a stiff nod and headed down the pathway.

Ellie headed inside to check on Rose one last time before

leaving for the evening. Though she couldn't see through Rose's kitchen window if Uncle Ross's horse was in the stable, she could see that the pasture was empty, and she hoped it meant he still had not returned. She opened the back door and cocked her head to listen for sounds that he had returned. Nothing.

In her kitchen, she checked the roasting chicken for doneness. Juices from the bird's breast ran clear, and she returned it to the still-warm oven. Maybe she would have an appetite later but not now. Not even the jar of her favorite tomato chutney coaxed her appetite.

She snugged the dishcloth tighter around the bread and, with the mundane tasks finished, sat down at the table, only then letting her mind wander. She conjured the image of Martin at the table laughing over some inanity, but when she tried to bring his face into focus, it wouldn't come and a new wave of sadness washed over her.

With leaden feet, she dragged herself up the stairs to the sanctity of their room. Her room. As it had been for the past seven months. Scooping up the stack of letters she had left on the bed earlier, she unfolded the three sheets and read again Martin's last words to her. It would be so easy to discount Theo. She wanted to reject it, the idea of Martin being murdered. . .and by her uncle. So repelling. But what reason would Theo have to lie? Though he had deserted, the emotion he had expressed over the loss of Bud showed the mental strain the fighting had taken on him. Even Martin showed signs of that strain. And Uncle Ross. . .

Everything swirled in her mind. Deliberately, she ripped the end of one of the other envelopes, needing to know what else Martin had to say. The date was one week before the letter he had been working on the night he'd met Theo. She opened the other two envelopes, each dated a week previous to the other. She smiled. He had told her while on furlough that it sometimes took him a week to finish one letter, then he would send three or four of them all at once.

She found the one dated in April, three weeks before his reported death. As she read, she noticed that the tone matched that of the last one she had received. He was worried and tired. Though he tried to keep his tone light, his agitation showed. The next letter revealed the source of his frustration.

Your uncle Ross isn't well liked, darling. He is cold to the men's needs and seldom hesitates in carrying out extreme punishment for the mildest infraction.

He made no other mention of Uncle Ross. Ellie wondered if his assessment of punishment was from personal experience or what he had witnessed. The next letter seemed more desperate.

Punishment is ramping up. Talk of desertion is more common as are rumors that the captain is drinking. Most know my relationship to the man and withdraw from me. Yet Ross seems to show mercy to no man, regardless of relationship.

Most nights I lie awake thinking of you and our home. Perhaps we should think of moving out to the farm. The peace of that place speaks to my soul even now.

Ellie lay down and rested her head on her arms. Martin's unhappiness colored his death in shades of cold gray, just as the idea of his being shot burned into her mind like a great black ball. She fought the weariness that pulled at her and closed her eyes with the promise that it would be for only a minute. Just enough time to pull herself together before Uncle Ross returned or Theo brought the wagon in.

*

Theo leaned his head against the wall of the barn. He flexed his fingers, noting the bluish tint to the skin from where he had pinched them between two of the boards as he stacked the wagon full to conceal the new wood of the false bottom. At least his fingers weren't broken, though the first joint on his middle finger was tighter and more painful than the others. Now all he had to do was get over to Ellie's.

As the breeze filtered through the thick branches of the evergreens that screened him from the main house, he closed his eyes to drink in the solitude. Working with his hands had felt good. Even hearing Libby's happy munching from the stall as he finished his project had given him a sense of home. How long had it been now? A year? Two? He'd requested a furlough several times, always denied.

But he didn't want to think about the war, knowing what thin ice he treaded by allowing his thoughts to shift that direction. What was wrong with him? He didn't understand his nightmares or why his hands shook so badly sometimes. And least of all, he couldn't understand why it was so difficult for him to control the memories.

Frustrated, Theo pushed away from the barn wall and decided to walk around the property. Ellie had a jewel here, though the buildings, as she had suggested, showed some damage.

Where had he been during the battle in Gettysburg? Hunkered down in the woods of West Virgina most likely. Waiting. Biding his time. He'd known the general plan for the South to push north, and his desertion and plans to find Ellie made his position particularly precarious. He'd waited for almost a month to make a move, even finding work on a farm where the people had never asked him questions. Maybe when he left he would return there instead of going west.

The fields surrounding Ellie's property remained unplowed for next year's crops, and he wondered at the losses the farmers had endured. In the distance, he spotted a small building beside a pond. The springhouse. It would be the place Ellie planned to hide the runaways.

He was headed in that direction when movement caught his peripheral vision. He turned his head toward the fields on his left, expecting to see a bright-colored bird, but it was a man. Probably out looking for trinkets left behind by the warring troops. But the suddenness with which the man had appeared, unobserved by him, shook him, and he lost his desire to explore further.

With the sun dipping in the west, he turned back to the barn. His gaze went over the loaded wagon. Libby stuck her head out of her stall and whinnied at him. He stroked the animal's nose. A bittersweet longing rose in him to be the young man he had been before the war. The carefree fellow who delighted in playing tricks on his newly wedded cousin and loved nothing more than breaking horses for the wealthier plantation owners to use as carriage horses. He'd known as soon as the war started and the destruction of the South began that things would never be the same.

Weariness pulled at him, but he resisted. Instead, he hitched Libby to the wagon. He turned the wagon and headed out the drive and out onto the road leading back to Gettysburg.

He forced himself to concentrate on the bright red blotch flying through the air, a cardinal, and its less gloriously colored mate. A rabbit hopped off the road and into the field. Libby's harness added a pleasant jangle to the air, and Theo pursed his lips to whistle a tune to match the rhythm of the horse's hooves.

As Libby leaned harder into the harness to get up a gentle hill, Theo's tune died. In the midst of another rise to his right, covered by trees, he could see at its edge a wagon. Two black men worked with shovels. Whether they dug around a knickknack they'd found or a body yet uninterred, Theo didn't really want to know. He turned his head away and slapped the reins against Libby's back to hurry her along.

He pulled up to Ellie's as the sun skimmed the western

horizon. Everything seemed still and quiet. He set the hand brake on the wagon and slipped to the ground. Libby knickered softly and arched her head, and he reached to run his hand over her velvet neck. Pain shot up his arm. He winced and studied the fingers of his right hand. The middle finger had swollen to twice its size, and the bluish bruise across his other fingers had become a ragged purple mark.

"Theo?"

He lifted his head, seeing Ellie standing on the back porch. He heard her repeat his name and the note of concern, and then, before he could focus again, he felt her hand on his arm.

"Why are you standing here?"

He stared into her eyes, concern pinching the place between her brows, and held out his hand for her inspection.

৯

Ellie felt a stab of anxiousness when she saw his fingers. "Oh!"

She couldn't believe the mottled mess he'd made of his fingers. "Come over to the porch and sit down so I can look at them." Ellie made sure he followed her then pointed to the place where he should sit and perched next to him. She gently lifted his hand, aware of the weight of it against hers and the rough feel of his palm flush with hers. She traced the length of his middle finger. She watched his expression for signs of pain. When she placed pressure on the upper half of his middle finger, his face paled and he tried to pull away.

"It might be broken," she said. "What did you do?"

He sat up straight, a little color flushing back into his cheeks. "I was stacking wood into the bed, and my fingers got smashed between two pieces. It'll be fine. I got here without a problem."

She frowned. "Anyone can guide a horse with one hand. I bet you used your left."

He shrugged, realizing his arguments would fall on deaf ears. He tried to pull away again.

She pulled back. "Stop it. You're acting like a child."

For the first time, he raised his gaze to meet hers. His gray eyes held a solemnity that caught her breath. And something else loomed there. . . . "You don't make me feel like a child."

Her breath caught in her throat, and she released his hand and pushed to her feet. "I've got to get some bandages." Realizing how abrupt she sounded, she tried to soften her tone. "You sit still. I'll be back."

eighteen

Ellie's thoughts swirled as she searched for an old sheet to rip into strips to bind Theo's fingers. She couldn't be sure that middle finger wasn't broken. She would have to have Martha look at it. Maybe Theo would let her touch it.

Her face grew hot when she recalled the roughness of his palms and the luminescent light firing his eyes before his last statement, asking something she didn't quite understand. Or maybe she did. She closed her eyes and released a sigh.

When she reached for the tin of cloves, she realized how much easier Theo's injury made their job. Taking him to see Martha wouldn't be questionable at all. The only danger left would be his lone drive out to the farm. But, she reasoned, if anyone questioned him or her, the fact that he was doing repairs at the farm for her would be a solid excuse for his presence there.

She mashed the cloves and chickweed then made a paste and hurried out the door. He still sat where she left him, his wide shoulders slumped. For a second, she felt sorry for him. He had done so much. Sacrificed himself for her. Brought her evidence of the truth, however unpalatable she found it. But was she ready to believe him over her uncle Ross?

Ellie touched his shoulder to let him know she was there. He raised his head as she sat next to him and collected his right hand. "Spread your fingers out."

He rested his hand on his thigh and spread his fingers.

Her face flamed. She wished she could take him inside where she wouldn't have to be quite so personal in order to wrap his finger. She debated leaving the job for Martha, but the injury must hurt, and he had done it while trying to help her.

"What's the paste for?" He lifted his hand from his thigh and held it out.

Relief spread through her at his action. She dabbed the dark paste onto his middle finger then the others. "A mixture of cloves and chickweed to bring down the swelling."

"You know herbs?"

When she tied the last knot, she shook her head. "Not really. Martha knows many, though. It's part of the reason why Dr. Selingrove, Rose's husband, finds Martha's help so invaluable."

"She didn't seem too talkative when I went to get her that night."

"She's shy."

Theodore spit out a laugh. "That's not the impression I got."

She crossed her arms and frowned. "Martha is a kindhearted woman with a real gift for healing, even if she hasn't had formal training." She regretted her defensive tone when all the lightheartedness left his expression.

"I meant no offense."

She shifted away from him and stared out at the dead garden. "No. I—I overreacted. It's been. . .quite a day."

A wagon rattled up the road, and they paused to watch its passage. The traffic on Breckinridge Street grew less as the day melted into evening.

Ellie felt a sickening dread in her stomach when she thought about Uncle Ross's inevitable return. He would be on horseback and they would be able to see him before he saw them, but it was the conversation she dreaded. How could she pretend she didn't know a thing? Yet Theo had said he wasn't sure it was Uncle Ross, just that the man looked a lot like him. Uncle Ross would never shoot someone in cold blood. Was it Martin's punishment for leaving camp? Cavorting with the enemy?

Theo's voice cut into her thoughts. "When I saw her at that

doctor's office, I thought she was a servant or something."

Ellie dragged herself back to the conversation. "And acting too good for a woman with black skin?"

Surprise lit his features. "Well, yes. I guess this Southern boy has a lot to learn. I worked with black men. Breaking horses for the rich."

"Did you pay them?"

"Never crossed my mind. We were friends, though, and they often spoke of horrors their kin endured at the hands of their owners."

"If you give the blacks a chance, you can learn a lot about laughter, perseverance, and God."

"God?"

Ellie warmed to her subject, weighing each word against her own untouchable sorrow. "I've seen so many of them come through here, their clothes little more than rags, scars on their backs, arms, even their faces. One slave had a brand mark on his cheek because he'd run away once before and gotten caught. The brand was his punishment, but it didn't stop him from trying again. One older man said the reason their skin was so black was because they'd been through a sight more fires than white folk, and though they got scorched, the good Lord never let them get burned up."

And if they could persevere through such pain, I should be able to as well.

❧

Theo took note of her tender smile as she recounted the story. "You've done a lot to help them. That shows a great deal of spirit on your part. I think the Lord would be pleased with you."

Ellie's eyes darted to his face then away. "Maybe."

"You've stayed true to something you believe in."

"Martin always believed that everyone had a gift. He was the one that first saw Martha's talent for herbs."

"But you don't do this for him. You do it for yourself."

She nodded and squinted into the setting sun. "I suppose I do. It's always been hard for me to see people hurt. Even during the battle here, Rose and I did our best to help the wounded. We went to the hospital every day. It was terrible."

How well he knew. The one time a bullet had grazed his scalp, his visit to the field hospital had been frightening. The sourness of infection, the moaning, the bugs... Those men did not have the gentle touch of a woman or the thoughtful care of clean bandages and homemade poultices. He let his gaze slide over Ellie's profile, and his chest tightened. And they most certainly didn't have the beauty to help them forget their wounds and ease the long, lonely days of recovery.

She faced him then, her gaze searching his. "You're feeling better."

He could only nod as emotion clutched him. "Yes, I am."

"I listened to many war stories from the men as they recovered." Her gaze skittered away from his face. "Martin told me a few." He saw the way her lips quivered and knew she struggled for composure.

"He told you about the things he saw?"

"Some."

He straightened his back, working out the kinks, and rubbed his bandaged hand. "If I were married, I think it would be hard for me to talk about everything. It would be the one place the war couldn't touch unless I let it in, so I'd try and keep the door shut as long as possible."

A lone tear slipped down her cheek, and she swiped it away like an errant fly. "But I wanted to help by sharing his burden."

She was showing him a part of her hurt that he could only hope to soothe in some small way. He wasn't sure he knew how, though. How could he wrap up the torment of watching his friends and fellow soldiers die and the patriotism that tore at him to stay and fight? And then there were the other complications. Leaving meant death. But if not killed, then forever walking in a cloud of shame. Or struggling with not being able to endure when others did. Martin had been the same haggard, war-torn man he himself was. The difference was Martin had stayed and died, and he had left and was dying in a very different way.

Ellie's hand on his arm brought him alert. Her fingers dug into his forearm. Following the line of her gaze, he saw the lone horseman and heard Ellie's whisper. "It's Uncle Ross."

nineteen

Uncle Ross took his time dismounting. He acknowledged Ellie and Theo by an upraised hand but seemed otherwise relaxed to Theo's eye.

Theo studied the man more closely as Ross led the horse into the barn, trying to remember. But he feared the passage of time and his own dislike for Ross had biased him.

"We should leave." Ellie jerked her head to indicate his bandaged hand. "I'll help you get Libby hitched up. Just stay calm."

"Sure." He grinned down at her.

"What?"

"I'm calm. And Libby never got unhitched." His eyes slid down to where her hand grasped his arm then back to her. His smile grew.

She shook her head. "Yes, I guess she is." He saw the sudden shift in her mood when she glanced at the barn. Tension squared her shoulders, and her voice came to him low and terse. "Are you sure, Theo?"

It took him a minute to understand the change in subject and absorb the real meaning of her question. Her eyes never left her uncle as he reappeared briefly then turned his back to close the barn doors. "All I can tell"—he pitched his voice low—"is that he looks familiar."

Uncle Ross strode up to them.

Ellie stood.

Theo remained where he was.

"Ellie, my dear, I'm bushed. I'll probably eat something then head straight to bed. We can talk tomorrow."

"I'm sorry, Uncle. Theo's finger looks broken. We—we were just getting ready to hitch up Libby and take him to see the doctor."

Uncle Ross slid a look over at Libby. "She is hitched." His gaze met Ellie's, brows raised. "And I thought Dr. Selingrove was fighting."

She gaped and pink suffused her cheeks. Theo had never seen her quite so rattled. "Yes, that's right. He is fighting, but he's not the only doctor in Gettysburg."

Ross's eyes flicked to Theo, his expression cold.

Theo raised his hand to prove to the man that the need was legitimate. "I think I broke something." He was proud of himself for maintaining the Yankee pronunciation.

Ross looked away. "Then I suppose I'll make myself at home."

"Your business went well, I hope?" Ellie asked.

"It did. Thank you. I'm in an even better position than I thought possible."

To Theo's eye, Ross's answer caused even greater strain to Ellie, evidenced by the stiffening of her back and the worry line between her eyes.

"Went by the farm today." Ross's expression became gentle. "It's looking a little run down. If you'd let me, I could hire someone to take care of the repairs."

"I've already hired someone."

Ross's nostrils flared, and his hard gaze flicked to Theo. "I see."

It was that stare, the set of the jaw, and the way the fading light of day hit the planes of his face that brought a flash of certainty to Theo. It had been Ross that night. He would stake his life on it.

Ellie pulled her skirts up slightly and motioned to Theo to follow her before setting off toward Libby. "I'll see you tomorrow morning, Uncle."

"Tomorrow morning? I wonder what Martin would say about your being out that late."

Ellie spun on her heel. "What is that supposed to mean?"

Theo felt the weight of Ross's gaze but he kept his own eyes on Ellie.

Ellie's eyes blazed hot. "Martin is dead, and Theo is my hired help."

Ross opened his mouth, not looking the least bit cowed.

Ellie cut him off. "Nothing more, *Uncle*. And I resent the implications of your statement. It might be best for you to find somewhere else to stay for the remainder of your visit. Snyder's Wagon Hotel is just down the street."

Ross held out his hands toward Ellie. "Now, Ellie. You misunderstood me. Let's talk about this."

"As you suggested, *Uncle*, morning would be a better time to talk." She didn't wait for a reply, and Theo could only admire the steel reserve of the woman as he followed her to the wagon.

When he helped her into the wagon then settled in beside her, he glanced at her profile. She seemed oblivious to everything. Her arms were wrapped around herself. "He was a little too sure of himself," she murmured.

"Is he normally suspicious like that?"

"What if he knows about you, Theo?" Her blue eyes clouded, her words came fast. "You could take a vow to the U.S. Government, then we'll have nothing to fear."

He guided Libby with his good hand. Ellie's statement made it sound so simple, yet he knew a simple vow would not be the end to the turmoil and memories that plagued him. He glanced at Ellie's profile, not having missed the "we" in her last statement. He wondered if she cared. Would she offer the solution if she didn't? He couldn't help a little grin of satisfaction.

The wagon squeaked and moaned down the road, the sounds loud in the stillness. "I thank you for defending me, ma'am," he drawled, hoping to tease her into relaxing.

"It's none of his business who I'm with. And you're my cousin anyway."

He turned toward her. "Really?"

"By marriage."

"Oh."

She put a hand down to brace herself on the seat and frowned up at him. "What do you mean, 'Oh'?"

"Just. . .oh." He pulled back on the reins to slow Libby for the turn into the narrow road beside the doctor's office and wondered if what she'd said meant she would never think of him beyond cousin status.

"Pull over toward the garden and stop."

He tried to see the garden area in the dark. There was no sign of movement. He wondered if the slaves even knew of his arrival. Ellie leaned close to him, and he felt her warm breath against his ear. "They've already been instructed what to do. Don't worry. By the time we're done here, they'll be in place. Don't let on that anything is different."

He dared to turn toward her before she had a chance to lean away from him. Her eyes flew to his in surprise. He gave her a lazy smile. "Thanks, cuz."

twenty

Ellie watched as Martha examined Theo's fingers, knowing that as she sat there the runaways were crawling into the wagon as pre-instructed by Martha. From the code Martha had given the previous night, Ellie had known the baby hadn't been born yet and where to place the wagon, but the impending birth would cause the woman great discomfort in the bumpy ride to the farm. Still, it couldn't be helped. At least there would be less likelihood of discovery if she gave birth out at the farm than if she were in the cellar of Dr. Selingrove's offices—provided her uncle didn't decide to pay the farm another visit. That he had been on the property at all, without her permission, irritated her.

Ellie found herself transfixed by the placid expression on Theo's face as Martha probed his fingers. She confirmed that the middle one was broken, the pressure of her fingers on the joint and the wince of pain on Theo's face lending credit to her diagnosis. Without informing Theo of her intentions, Martha's strong fingers cupped around his middle finger and yanked.

Theo released a grunt then inhaled sharply.

Martha didn't even glance his way but set about putting herbs in a mortar and pestle. Ellie watched as she ground the herbs, noting that Theo remained quiet though collected.

She wished she could read his thoughts. Was he considering her suggestion? Was it because of what he had revealed about Uncle Ross that she felt such a need to protect him? Or was it because protecting him meant protecting her own secret?

For a fleeting moment, in the wagon, she had thought he

might kiss her. When he had only smiled and commented about being her cousin, her disappointment had been palpable. Worse, she'd felt every bit the fool for thinking such thoughts.

When Theo turned his head and caught her staring at him, another flush of heat went through her. After tonight she wouldn't see him as much. Returning to the mundane tasks of living and taking care of Rose would make things easier. She could grieve uninterrupted.

If Theo stayed out at the farm, there would be plenty of work for him to do for a couple of weeks. Then, instead of having him do the necessary repairs on her house, she would pay him and encourage him to leave. Thank him for all he had done and release him. If he didn't take the vow, he would continue his journey, running from his responsibility.

Embers of anger stirred over that thought. How could he look at himself knowing he had deserted the cause for which Bud and all his other friends fought? If only it had been Martin to come back to her instead of Theo. . .

&

At the farm, Theo backed the wagon to the barn and left it there as Ellie had instructed him. He would stay in the stable for two nights, then the springhouse would be his until he finished the repairs. According to Ellie's racing monologue on the way back to her house, she would then pay him and he could leave. His services no longer needed. And the whole time Ellie spouted the litany of instructions, she hadn't once looked him full in the face.

He worked the straps to unhitch Libby. "Some oats should help ease the workload you had today, huh, girl?" If only his own load could be erased so easily. He led the horse into the barn and closed the doors, leaving the runaways to do whatever it was they'd been instructed to do.

He didn't begin to understand Ellie's strange withdrawal from him but attributed it to the lateness of the hour and everything he had shared with her that day. She would need some time and space to process everything. The farm and the work would keep his mind off her. Maybe she would change her mind and ask him to stay, but he had to be prepared if she didn't. Could be she realized having him around was too big a risk to her own safety.

Libby pawed the ground when she saw the bag of oats he was preparing. The horse's happy crunching didn't cover the low mewling that came to his ears. He stilled. The runaways must be making their move through the field to the springhouse.

If prayer changed things, he prayed for freedom for the couple and their baby to come. He'd often given thought to the things he and his friends held dear and the way of life that called upon them to fight to preserve what was familiar. Many of his unit struggled between the knowledge that they fought for the entire South, even as their homes and hometowns struggled to survive.

Thoughts of home brought an ache and anger, but he let them go. Had to. Did he have a right to be angry at the destruction when he had deserted? He hadn't fought so much for his home state's right to have slaves as much as his right to have a home unsullied by war.

Theo spread a layer of hay in the stall next to Libby's and stretched out. A piece jabbed him in the cheek as he turned his head to get comfortable and raised his arms to pillow his head. His muscles relaxed, but his mind raced with problems, and every problem seemed to lead to Ellie's image burned in his mind, beautiful and kindhearted. And alone.

Like him.

At some point in the night, he was startled awake. He rubbed a hand over his eyes and blinked into the darkness. Used to a nightmare waking him, he recalled nothing remotely frightening tearing away his sleep. On the edge of his awareness, though, he recalled something.

He rose to his knees then to his feet, moving quietly lest he miss whatever sound woke him. Libby remained quiet in her stable, a lone ear pricked in his direction as he moved through the barn.

He pushed the wooden bar back and swung the door out enough to slide through the opening. Cold swept over him, stealing his breath. Stars shone brightly from the heavens. Everything seemed still and in its place.

Theo turned in the direction of the springhouse. Though he couldn't see it from the barn, he wondered if the runaways were doing well. Maybe the woman had given birth and the sound of the baby had woken him. He frowned. No, that didn't seem quite right.

Frustrated, he ducked back inside and settled down in the hay, still warm from his body.

twenty-one

Ellie woke with a headache and a vague feeling of unease. She pulled herself up in bed and squinted into the blush of light coming through the eastern bedroom window. Everything rushed back to her in a flood. Martin's letters. Uncle Ross's persistence. Theo's suspicions about her uncle. And thoughts of Theo brought other memories. The intensity of his gray gaze on her. The way he had said she didn't make him feel like a child. His silly grin down at his arm where she had clutched it while insisting that Libby needed hitched. How her breath caught at the sight of him.

Infatuation. He was a man. She was a woman. And she was alone.

Confused by what it all meant, Ellie leaned to grab the letters on the table beside her bed. She fingered the paper, its stiffness and smooth texture, but it was Martin's bold script that mesmerized her. She expected the sting of sorrow at the sight, surprised when the emotional tidal wave did not come. She sifted through each of the letters, sad that she would never be able to say good-bye to Martin and that she would never hear his booming laughter again.

She went over the passages that referred to Uncle Ross, puzzled by the changes in her uncle. He had been by her mother's side as the months had drained away her strength. Yet Ellie couldn't deny that even her mother seemed unsure of Uncle Ross before she died.

One occasion in particular rose from dusty memories. About a week before her mother had slipped into unconsciousness, Uncle Ross had stayed with her the entire day. Ellie never knew what they talked about, but she did know that her mother was troubled. "He is not the brother I once had," had been the simple comment.

At the time Ellie hadn't thought much of her mother's observation, but now, in light of Martin's letters and Theo's revelation, she recalled other things. Her mother's agitation. Her desire to see Alex Reeves, her attorney. The general exhaustion in her mother's face and the red-rimmed eyes. Perhaps the most telling element of all was that Uncle Ross never returned to see her mother again, even avoiding the funeral with a wire that he was up north.

Muddled with all the problems on her plate, Ellie determined to get up and moving. She would check on Rose and baby Colin, then. . .

What?

Theo's face flashed in her mind, and she wondered if he would have everything he needed for repairs. Even if he did, it might be a good thing to check on the runaways. If the woman had given birth, she might need some things, though she doubted Martha would have allowed the woman to leave her ever-watchful eye without supplying her with the basic needs.

Her thoughts toiled and tumbled over each other as she washed and dressed. She scrambled eggs, and the yellow and white mass matched her mindset. She sat to eat and bit her lip when she thought of Martin sitting in the chair across from her all those months ago. Then Theo's presence. She shook away the images and hurried through her breakfast. After finishing, she prepared a fresh mound of eggs and a slice of ham for Rose to eat.

When she slipped into Rose's kitchen, though, her friend was busy at the stove, the smell of bacon and coffee hanging in the air.

"You're up!"

Rose turned, her house dress swirling around her legs. Her eyes were bright and her smile relaxed. "I was so tired of being in bed I thought it best to get up and move around. And I was hungry."

Ellie raised the covered plate. "I brought you scrambled eggs and a nice slice of ham."

Rose's laughter trilled across the room and she pointed to the plate beside her on the counter. It held a mound of eggs and four strips of bacon. "I'll probably eat both plates."

Happy to see her friend in such good spirits, Ellie picked up baby Colin from his cradle while Rose, true to her word, polished off both meals. "If I continue to eat like this, I'll be twice the size as when Robert left."

Ellie rubbed her finger down the soft cheek of Colin's face. "Robert would be so glad to see you, he wouldn't care."

"He might if he has to buy me a wardrobe of new dresses."

There was a hope in Rose's words that had been missing lately. "Have you had news?"

Rose leaned forward to gather Colin into her arms. "No. But I've prayed and felt such a peace over it all that I'm certain he'll be home."

Ellie had felt the same way for so long. Then the news of Martin's death had shaken her. Hard.

"Where's Theo?"

"Out at the farm doing some repairs."

"Are you going out to see him? He's probably hungry. Take a plate for him."

Ellie thought Rose's tone had a suggestive lilt, but when she glanced at her friend, she was busy rearranging the blanket around Colin. "I had thought about making sure he had all he needed for the repairs." Food hadn't occurred to her for a minute. She would make a number of sandwiches and take some apples over to him. After that he would have to fend for himself.

"Are you still thinking of selling to your uncle?" Rose lifted the baby to her shoulder and patted his back.

"Why, no, of course not. I've never given it serious thought. It's only that Uncle Ross is so stubborn that he won't take no for an answer."

"Why do you suppose that is?"

"I wish I knew."

"Does Theo like it out there?"

Ellie thought it a strange question. "I don't know."

"It's safer for him at the farm."

She had to concur.

"You're lonely without him."

Ellie sucked in a breath and met her friend's steady gaze. "Rose," she breathed, "I'm a widow."

Her friend's lips curved into a soft smile. "You're a woman first, Ellie. And Martin would want you to love again."

"I could never think of Theo in that way. He's my cousin."

Rose's smile grew wider. "Only by marriage, and I think you've been thinking of him that way since he arrived."

Ellie gulped air and shot to her feet. "How could you say such a thing?"

Rose pulled Colin from her shoulder, looking not the least bit flustered by Ellie's protest. "Because I'm a woman, and I've seen him look at you that same way."

"Rose!" was all she could say in protest.

Her friend widened her eyes mockingly. "Ellie!"

"I don't believe this. I made a vow to Martin to love him and honor him. How could you think. . . ?"

Rose was nodding. "It's true. You've kept your vows."

Ellie stilled, mollified.

Rose's smile was back. "But you forgot a very important detail."

A protest rose to Ellie's lips.

" Till death do you part. He's gone, Ellie."

All the air left Ellie's lungs, and she flopped back in the chair, shaken by her friend's words. She loved Martin. Theo could never take his place, but Rose's other suggestion niggled at her. Did Theo really look at her in that way? Beyond admiring his eyes and admitting how much nicer he looked clean shaven, had she thought about him in *that* way?

She stiffened, appalled at the plunge her thoughts had taken.

"Martin would want you to move on and be happy again. I can't think of anyone better than his best friend."

Ellie spat a sigh. "What are you trying to do?" Her eyes sheened over. "How can I just—"

She jerked to her feet.

Rose stood as well, a stricken expression on her face.

Ellie shrugged past her friend and out the back door. The sobs built in her throat. She hurried across the porch to her door and slammed it open, the first tormented cry ripping from her throat.

❧

The knock on the door grew louder, and Ellie wondered at her visitor's determination. Uncle Ross could knock until he fell over; she wouldn't answer. It couldn't be Rose since she was on her feet and obviously feeling better.

She rolled onto her back and stared up at the ceiling in her bedroom as another knock echoed up the stairs. It must be serious. Maybe Rose had taken sick. Or Colin. Unable to stand it another minute, Ellie hurried down the stairs and to the back door, throwing it open.

Martha stood there, her black face tense, her eyes solemn. "How's that man's finger doing?"

She hardly had time to stand aside before the woman pushed by her. This was not like Martha. Something was going on and she was using Theo's broken finger as a diversion in case she had visitors. Ellie gave the door a shove and faced her friend. "It's safe. Uncle Ross is not here."

Martha nodded. "One of the conductors was caught. Most of the people got away. They were sent here, but there's no room for them."

"Theo is at the farm, and Uncle Ross is staying elsewhere tonight. The cellar would work."

But Martha was shaking her head. "You don't understand. There's great risk. These people were almost caught and might still be followed. It's dangerous to have them in town."

"The farm?"

"It's what I hoped you might be offerin'. There's eight of them."

"Eight!" Panic edged up Ellie's spine. They would never be able to get eight people into the concealed part of the wagon.

"They'll do what needs done. You know that."

She did know that. She had heard stories of blacks huddled in crates, enduring all manner of rocky roads and dusty trails, not to mention stifling heat, freezing cold, and awkward positions, if it meant gaining their freedom. "When?"

"Not tonight but tomorrow. We'll use the usual signal. Do you think that man will help us, and can he be trusted?"

"Theo?" Ellie realized with a sinking heart that the situation was dire. Even if she didn't want to see him again and rebelled at the idea of taking food over in light of Rose's observations, the decision to see him was being taken out of her hands. She would have to make the trip now. To trust him for help and secrecy. Why did that make her afraid? Ellie ran her hands down the front of her dress then raised her chin. "Yes. I'll talk to him, and I'll leave the signal tonight if all is well."

Martha's dark eyes snapped to a point beyond Ellie's shoulder.

Ellie's flesh raised, and a cold chill breathed against her skin.

Martha's words came out slow and distinct. "You change his bandage and apply the poultice." Though Martha spoke of Theo's fingers, her eyes signaled caution to Ellie. The woman mimed for her to open the door as she continued. "You checked on Miss Rose?"

Ellie nodded that she understood and put her hand on the doorknob. "She was up and about at breakfast. She said she felt good, and Colin seemed content."

Martha dug her hand into an apron pocket and held out a small package. "I made up some more poultice for his fingers." She pressed it into Ellie's hands and gestured for her to open the door.

Ellie realized with a sinking feeling that the door had not caught when she went to shut it, but the greater horror gripped her as she swung the door inward to reveal her uncle Ross standing on the porch, his stony gaze broken suddenly by a huge smile. "Good evening, Ellie."

twenty-two

"I was just leaving, Uncle Ross," Ellie blurted. His smile didn't wilt a bit, and that in itself heightened Ellie's nerves. Steeling herself, she turned to Martha and floundered for the direction of the conversation before she had opened the door to Uncle Ross.

Martha pointed to the small parcel. "Listen good, now. Apply it to his fingers and wrap them tight." She pushed forward and Uncle Ross fell back a couple of steps to let Martha by, acknowledging her with the merest nod.

Ellie dreaded what it was he might have heard. She dared to pray that God would protect their deeds from Uncle Ross.

"I'm so sorry to interrupt." His smile seemed forced now. "I wasn't sure you would be home, though I'm glad you are. Is Rose doing well?"

Ellie struggled with how to react. Should she show her irritation at his interruption, or would that anger him? Yet she couldn't quite find the strength to be the dutiful niece. "Rose is fine," was all she could manage.

"If you would invite me in, I would like to talk to you."

She tried a smile to match his own. "As I said, I was just leaving."

"But your wagon isn't here. I checked."

The knowledge angered her. "I'm sorry, but I don't see what right you have to be in my barn."

His smile fell into a firm line. "I was looking to assure myself that you might be in. When I didn't see your wagon, I assumed you weren't. I'm certainly glad I didn't leave right away." He took one step closer to her. "I think I must have offended you

117

somehow. In my diligence to offer my services to help you at this terribly hard time in your life, I overstepped myself and made it appear I thought you incapable of managing."

The farm. It was always about the farm. Staring into his face, she saw vestiges of the kindhearted man she'd known since a child, and the slightest doubt crept in that Theo might have been wrong.

"You're a very capable young woman, just as your mother was quite capable. The truth is, my dear—" He paused and glanced around, as if embarrassed. For the briefest moment his eyes landed on Martha as she cleared the gate that led back to her home. "I have a very fond place for the old farm. I would like to manage the rents for it and, if you would consider it, perhaps carve out a couple of acres for myself. It would please me greatly to be close to family again. You are all that I have left."

Ellie hesitated at the earnestness in his eyes. Touched by his sincerity, she reminded herself that he was all she had left as well. In the lines around his face, she could see the family resemblance. Her mother's cleft was her uncle's as well as her own. And living at the farm had been her dream when the promise of children had been alive. Martin's death changed all that. Other than her own memories of the place, there was no longer a reason to hold on to the land. The crops had been ruined from the battle. She could notify the farmers that rented the land that it was being sold.

But still Ellie hesitated. She couldn't bring herself to say the words. She couldn't totally dismiss Theo's story. Martin had been Theo's cousin and best friend. What would be the point of his making up such a thing? Her stomach twisted with stress. Who did she believe? If she told her uncle Theo's story, would he simply laugh and deny the charge, or would those dark eyes become murderous?

She wrapped her arms around herself to mask the shudder of fear.

Uncle Ross shifted his weight and placed his forearm against the door frame. "It is a chilly night. Look, I can see that you need some time. It just so happens that I'll be here a little longer than I thought. Why don't I come by tomorrow evening and we'll discuss more of the details."

Her stomach tightened. She wondered if he had heard the conversation between her and Martha. Wondered if the extension of his time in Gettysburg was connected somehow to what he'd heard if he'd been listening at the door.

But he wouldn't know about her activities. How could he? Besides, he was a Northerner. Surely he would sympathize with what she was doing. If he had heard, they still had no choice but to go forward with their plans. With the number of blacks needing to be hidden there was no way they could use the cellar. Martha would know that as well. It had to be the farm. Uncle Ross wouldn't harm them.

She met Uncle Ross's dark eyes and wondered why, then, she felt so afraid.

&

Theo lowered his arms and rested his back. The constant pounding on the loose boards that made up the fence surrounding the barn and house had left his shoulders tense and his back sore. His broken finger throbbed, but he kept on. Without an official list of repairs, he had eyeballed the various buildings and picked the tasks he would undertake based on the tools he had available.

He'd kept an ear cocked toward the springhouse all morning, wondering about the couple. Hoping they had made it into the secret compartment of the wagon and not entirely sure they had. How could they be so quiet? What if they hadn't made it at all? Or if they had arrived late? He had no way of knowing whether they were there or not, and it troubled him.

He'd told himself a million times that he was better off not knowing and not getting involved. Still. . .

Theo gripped the hammer tighter and knelt to fix the lower boards. His stomach growled a protest, and he swallowed a gulp of water he'd fetched from the pond at the springhouse. He needed food, and he would need more nails soon, too. If Ellie wanted the farmhouse siding repaired, he would need planks and paint, and if she wanted stonework on the barn fixed, he would need sand and lime and some hand tools. Maybe if he did a great job, she would relent and let him stay on to help fully restore the buildings. By then he would know if she would be capable of returning his love.

He screamed out in pain as the hammer came down on his thumb. He popped the mashed digit into his mouth and sucked. Served him right for letting his mind wander to business that wasn't his. He sank to the ground and pulled out his thumb. Purple. And swelling. Fast. He grimaced at the sight and twisted around at the sound of a horse clopping closer. When he cupped his hand over his eyes, he could make out the form of a woman in the saddle.

He waited as Ellie came up the dirt lane toward the barn. Her coldness the previous evening left him unsure of how to approach her, or even if he should.

He turned back to the loose board, lifted it into place, and began to sink the nail. In his mind, he traced the path she would take to reach him, if indeed she had come to speak to him. She might have come to collect rent or check on the runaways. But no, she wouldn't have come down the dirt lane toward the barn. For rent she would have gone to the house. And for the runaways she could have cut across the field.

He tried to wring her from his thoughts by pounding hard and fast. The nail sunk in three strikes, his broken finger throbbed from clutching the hammer so tight, and his purple thumb on the opposite hand beat its own pained protest. He got to his feet, tempted to look over his shoulder but forcing himself to focus on the fence. He checked the next board and found it stable and firm.

"Theo?"

Despite his desire to remain aloof, the sound of her voice tripped the rhythm of his heart. He took his time straightening and finally turned to face her with a thin smile and a casual, "Howdy, boss."

twenty-three

Ellie caught Theo's glances as she directed Rose's horse up the dirt lane to the barn. Her stomach tickled with nervousness as she neared him. His back to her, wide as any wall, effectively separating them. She dismounted and took a step closer, stopping when he faced her and ground out his flippant greeting.

The planes of his face were hard, his mouth without the usual good-natured smile. But his eyes were what she didn't understand. The gray light of his gaze was cold. "I—I came to see if there was anything you needed. And to bring you something to eat," she hastened to add.

His eyes raked over her, bold and careless. "Now why would you think I need anything? I'm just a Rebel without responsibility or care."

His flippant attitude stung her, confirming her fears that he could be the liar and her uncle the innocent victim. If he could act like this to her, what made him incapable of being a vicious liar bent on destroying. . . Who? What? Her heart raced, and she couldn't catch her breath. She took a quick step backward, closer to the horse.

He closed the distance between them and grasped her forearm, his fingers a gentle band of iron. "Ellie, forgive me. I. . ." His gaze commanded her attention, gray eyes searching, no longer remote and cold.

"Let me go!"

He did and she slid away from him, closer to the dappled gray. She stroked the horse's neck, her back to him. She had come for some measure of reassurance. Evidence that her trust in him had not been ill placed, and she had gotten coldness. Anger. Why was he angry?

When she finally found the strength to turn, she avoided looking at him on purpose. She moved to the saddlebags and retrieved the food. She set it on the rock and forced herself to say something. Anything. "If you'll give me. . .a list"—the quiver in her voice could not be quelled—"I'll get what you need."

But the other matter pressed on her. She could not leave without asking for his help. She brought air into her lungs in an effort to still her fears. The horse's warmth beckoned to her. She could pull herself into the saddle and leave, but Martha's news meant she needed him. At least until tomorrow night, then she would tell him to leave. Rose had been wrong about him, and the thought brought a hollow ache to Ellie's heart.

She stiffened her spine, finally locking on his face.

ঞ

Theo allowed her the time to think things through. When she had turned back to him instead of riding off, hope burgeoned that she would be quick to forgive. She didn't immediately say anything, and every throb of his thumb and ache of his broken finger ticked off the seconds of her silence.

When at last she met his gaze, he dared to speak. "I'll get a list together."

Tension seemed to ebb from her shoulders at his simple answer. He chided himself for being so careless with her but acknowledged his own hurt feelings. "Last night. . ." He wondered if she really wanted to hear his explanation but forged ahead. "You were so quiet. Then when you told me I should leave in a couple of. . ."

She bit her lip and stared down at her feet. "I brought more poultice for your finger."

Hadn't she heard a word he'd said? "You really want me to leave, Ellie?"

Her eyes slid shut, and she dug a hand into the pocket at her waist and pulled out a small package. "Why don't you sit down on that rock and let me look at your finger."

Without pushing the issue further, he retreated to the rock and sat. She blinked in the sunlight, seemingly shocked that he had obeyed her request. With growing impatience, he lifted his hand and began work on the bandage, but his injured thumb was too swollen and clumsy. He groaned at the stabbing pain and she was there, by his side.

"What did you do now?"

He grinned up at her, drinking in her concern, the soft curls that framed her face.

As she captured his hand in hers, she sat beside him and began inspecting the swollen, darkening thumb. "How. . . ?"

"Hit it knocking in a board."

"I would think you would learn to be more careful."

"I was being careful, but I got distracted."

She pulled his hand closer, clearly exasperated. "What on earth is there out here to distract you?"

She unwrapped the bandage and laid it aside, her fingers stroking along the edges of his thumb. The sensation of warmth and the tickle of her touch filled his senses. "Nothing."

She leveled a glare on him, eyebrows raised. "Then what?"

"I was thinking about you."

He saw panic rise in the depths of her blue eyes, and she turned her face away. "I'm a married woman, Theo."

"You're a widow," he whispered.

She gave a nervous laugh. "Rose said the same thing."

He lifted his free hand to her chin and brought her face back so he could see into her eyes. Confusion settled in her gaze, and something else. . .fear. He wanted to erase both of those emotions. He would test the waters first. "I can leave in two weeks if you'd like."

A flash of emotion sparked in her eyes, and he wanted to

believe it was because her feelings were matching his. She opened her mouth, but no sound came out.

He leaned in, forcing her to pull away or surrender.

"It's too soon, Theo."

"Too soon for what?"

She swallowed hard, her lips trembling. "For this."

"For a conversation?" he teased.

She shook her head, the warm smoothness of her cheek rubbing against his palm.

"For what, then?" He could see evidence of the war within her, the longing to love again and the chains that bound her to the memory of Martin.

"A gentleman would understand and—"

He brushed his thumb over her lips to stop the flow of words. He could feel the pulse in her neck that matched his own racing heart. He lowered his head and smiled into her eyes, whispering the words. "I'm a Rebel, remember?"

Her soft exhale blew warm against his face, and he closed the distance between them. Her lips, so soft. Her hair silky beneath his hand. And when he pulled away and she opened her eyes, he saw the beginning of something new shining there.

twenty-four

So many emotions crashed around in Ellie's mind. Anger at herself. Fear of letting Martin go. Terror at the desire that propelled her to want Theo to kiss her. But his lips smoothed all the knots of her distress. The feel of his fingertips along her jaw and the innate gentleness of his lips, only when he pulled back did she breathe and float back to reality. His eyes held mischief, and his lips pursed in a knowing little grin that brought a rush of heat to her cheeks. She would have turned away, but his hand still cupped her face.

"I didn't come here to fall in love, Ellie." His gaze, steady now, all humor gone, sucked her in.

She closed her eyes and bit her lower lip. "What about Martin?"

Theo's deep chuckle surprised her. When she opened her eyes, his were luminous. "You love the memories you made together, the love you shared, and you make sure there's room in your heart for me." He leaned away from her and winced.

She remembered his broken finger, the poultice, and Martha. "Here." She reclaimed his hand with the swollen thumb in her own, trying to absorb all that had happened in the last few minutes and figure a way to shift the conversation to the runaways.

"Yes, boss," he ribbed.

They shared a laugh.

"Ellie?"

"Hmm?" She rubbed the poultice over his thumb.

"When did you find out about Martin?"

"About a month before the Confederates arrived here."

"So you were still helping the runaways despite your own hurt."

"Yes. I wanted to help them. After I found out about Martin..." The pang his name invoked was dull. Guilt stabbed momentarily at the kiss she'd just shared with a man other than her husband.

Rose's admonition tugged at her. *But you forgot a very important detail—till death do us part. He's gone....*

"Ellie?"

She focused on him. This man. Her lips still warm from his kiss. She realized for the first time in a long time that maybe God hadn't abandoned her. Her own stubborness and, yes, bitterness, had robbed her of hope. Her gaze went to the sky. He was there. Waiting.

I am so sorry.

Theo's hand moved in hers, and she felt the touch of his fingers along her cheek. "I didn't mean to make you cry."

She shook her head. "No, no. It's just... I realized something important."

His eyes searched hers, a question there, but he didn't ask.

She looked away.

"You were saying about your work with the blacks."

He was giving her some space, and she was grateful. "Martha talked to me about it. She and I grew up together, and I couldn't imagine a world in which black people were treated as, well, as property. She told me stories of her kin in the South. Then one night she needed help and asked me if she could use my cellar. I've helped ever since." She shifted away from him and scooped some of the poultice from the wrapping. She felt the hard calluses of his hands and tried to remember what Martin's hands had felt like. She couldn't. "I read Martin's letters."

"It must have been hard to see his writing after so long."

She gave him a quick smile and concentrated on wrapping

his finger. "Yes. Very hard, but it was...I don't know...healing somehow. But that's not what I wanted to tell you." She raised her gaze to his. "Martin mentions Uncle Ross several times. I get the impression that he was careful how he said things, probably because he knew Ross was my uncle, but his last letter indicated that Uncle Ross was acting strangely."

Theo inclined his head. "Go on."

"There wasn't much else. He went on to express his disgust with the war and how much he just wanted to come home." The telling and Theo's closeness made her waver from her earlier conviction that Uncle Ross might be the victim. Or was the kiss distracting her from seeing the truth? How was it Uncle Ross could be innocent? How could she doubt Theo? He'd risked so much to get to her.

"Most of the men just want to go home, Ellie."

⁓

"You did?" Her gaze held no guile, but the question begged more than a pat answer. It wasn't hard for him to find the words.

"You feel trapped. You're expected to kill on a daily basis at the whim of a man you only hear about." He firmed his jaw, the old anger coming back. "You march for miles with little food then sleep in a tent if you're lucky enough to have one."

He watched her tie a small knot in the fresh bandage. She waggled her fingers, indicating he should let her look at his other hand. She unwrapped and examined the broken finger and began to rub fresh poultice over it. He wanted to tell her it didn't hurt as much but figured there was no reason to, being that he enjoyed her closeness. Her touch.

"Then there are actual battles, where men you've become friends with die right beside you, blown to bits or shot up so bad..." His mouth went dry, and he felt the now-familiar chill of nerves. "You can't imagine what it's like."

"I think I can." Then softer, "Why did you leave?"

Hadn't his explanation made it obvious?

"I mean, why did you risk everything to come here to tell me about Martin when you could have gone west and written it out in a letter?"

Theo stared down as she finished wrapping his finger. "It was the only place I could think to go, and I knew if the roles were reversed, if Martin had lived and I had died, I would have wanted him to be there for my wife."

She lifted his hand and twined her fingers in his, an unexpected gesture that should have sent a warning signal that the next question might rattle his world. "What if you're caught?"

He tilted his face toward the sun, stretching the muscles in his neck and squeezing her hand, knowing the answer to the question and suspecting she did as well. "I'll be shot."

They sat side by side for a long time before she released his hand and began wrapping up the rest of the poultice. "Uncle Ross came to me this morning."

"About this place?"

She stared at the fields stretched out to their right. He followed her gaze where, in the distance, a lone man and a small boy walked, probably looking for relics. It was the same man he'd seen before, probably explaining to his grandson the reason why his father wasn't coming home.

"He confused me."

Theo waited. There was more, he was sure.

"It made me doubt your intentions and wonder if Uncle Ross might be innocent." She patted the pocket wherein lay the package of poultice. "I got so mixed up."

"What changed that?"

"I don't know."

But he suspected her reaction to *him*, their kiss, had confused matters in her mind.

"Before he arrived, Martha was with me. There's a group of

runaways. Some of them were caught and the others escaped. They're scared, and Martha needs a place large enough for them all. I offered the farm."

It flitted through his mind that the kiss was just her way of getting him to help her, but he rejected the suspicious idea before it had a chance to take root.

"Martha began to act strangely, and we discovered that the door hadn't been closed all the way. When I went to open it—"

"Your uncle was on the other side."

Her eyes went huge. "How did you know?"

"Guessed. Where is he now?"

She stood, and he slipped off the rock as well and followed. She moved her eyes along the fence he had repaired, running her hand against the now-straight line of boards. "I told him I would have a decision for him, and he's coming back tomorrow evening."

"When do we need to transfer the runaways?"

"Tomorrow evening. Late. Martha will give me the signal if all is well, and I'm supposed to let her know tonight whether we're clear to use the farm."

"You mean whether or not I agreed to help."

She sent him a brief, sheepish smile. "Well, yes."

He had to know. "Didn't you just say you were afraid to trust me?" He had thought he glimpsed emotion in her eyes after their kiss, but if she couldn't trust him now, with all he had risked for her, he wondered if she ever could. Or maybe he was being unfair to expect so much. Maybe the better question was did he want to risk his heart to a woman who might not return it to him whole?

twenty-five

Ellie waited as Theo made a list of things he needed for the work on the buildings around the farm. She tried hard not to admire his profile or the way his hair curled on his neck or the remembered touch of his hand on her jaw or the look in his clear, gray eyes after he had kissed her. She hugged herself, more pleased than she could have imagined, refusing, for this moment, to let the doubts assail her.

Theo, leaning against the rock and using the surface to write on, caught her movement and sent her a wink that made her catch her breath. "Think we're almost done here."

She walked to Rose's dappled gray and stroked the horse's neck to take her mind off the man. She couldn't help but see the irony of her situation. To feel such things for another man so soon after Martin's death. . . Yet it had been seven months. A year total, she realized, since his furlough late in 1862. The last time she had held him. Was it right to feel so strongly about someone else so soon, or was she fickle? She tried to imagine Rose's response and knew her friend would tell her to embrace the moment. She would point out the fact that Mrs. Emma Bradley and Mrs. Louise Shevring had both remarried since the death of their husbands at Gettysburg. True, Mrs. Bradley had remarried a man much older than herself, but Mrs. Shevring, now Mrs. Nelson, had married a Union soldier who had hidden in her home at one point in the Gettysburg battle. Did every widow feel such a sense of guilt about moving on?

"Ellie?"

She started, Theo's hand on her arm steadying her.

"I didn't mean to scare you." His eyes crinkled at the corners, and his smile was lazy.

"I didn't expect you to be done so soon."

"It was harder to write, but I managed." He held out the paper.

She accepted the sheet with trembling fingers and turned to collect the reins of the gray. Without her mounting block she would need to find a surface high enough from which to mount. She clicked for the gray to follow her and led him toward the rock she'd used previously.

"Need a hand?" Theo appeared beside her. "You need only ask, my lady."

Ellie glanced between the rock and Theo and wondered if she could stand being so close to him again. Would he press her for another kiss or could she escape. Did she want to?

Without waiting for an answer, Theo took the reins from her hand and brought the horse in closer to the rock. He grasped her waist and swung her up to the rock and climbed up beside her.

She arched a brow. "You could have just given me a leg up."

"Naw, this is much more fun."

Heart pounding, she made sure the horse was in position. He waited for her to arrange her skirts then pulled her closer where they stood inches apart. Before she had a chance to draw another breath, his hands went to her waist and he picked her up.

She gasped. "Theo!"

He set her down on the sidesaddle. "There now, you're ready to ride. Except one thing."

Head swirling, she shot him a look and shifted to settle herself, looping her leg around the pommel.

He leaned toward her, creating a shadow over her face, and planted a tender kiss on her forehead.

Words jammed into her throat, waiting to be spoken. She gulped air and groped for something else to say. "You'll go into town tonight to pick up the supplies?"

His grin was crooked. "Yes, boss."

❧

Theo watched her wheel the horse around. She glanced over her shoulder at him then tapped the horse's flank with the crop.

He'd been tempted to plant that last kiss on her lips but thought it might be pushing her too hard. If she'd known the intensity of his feelings, no doubt she would have run and hidden. Even he hadn't known how much she had gotten under his skin until he had seen the light in her eyes upon pulling away from their kiss.

Lord, keep me strong.

He picked up his hammer and returned to driving new nails into the board fence or pounding the loose ones in. It was boring work. Lonely. He'd welcomed the lonesomeness after leaving camp. Having been surrounded for so long by shouting men, the sounds of cannon and gunfire, or the bugle corps, solitude appealed to him. But now, with the taste of Ellie's kiss still on his lips, he became aware of a need for something more.

As she had suggested, he could take the oath of the U.S. Government and settle down to farming. If not in Gettysburg, maybe Ellie would go west with him.

He worked out his plans as he hammered then added to them as he went into town to fetch the supplies. The south road into town seemed busier than usual. He felt the stares of the older men at the store and knew they wondered who he was and where he'd come from. Keeping his mouth shut as much as possible, he made sure to limp as he loaded the wagon. At last, he turned the wagon and headed north, back to the farm, his heart lighter than he could remember it being for a long time.

twenty-six

Ellie glanced up at the back of Dr. Selingrove's office in the distance, to the second floor, barely visible, where Martha had a little room. She unlatched the iron gate and swung it wide, latching it so it could not be easily shut, then crossed her backyard to knock on Rose's door. From the security of her second-floor room, Martha would see the signal that all was going as planned.

The kitchen area was empty, though a plate gave evidence that Rose hadn't been down since breakfast. She hurried upstairs, afraid to find Rose in the midst of a raging fever because she'd done too much too soon. The stillness of the little house seemed heavy, eerie. She gave a light knock on Rose's door before peering through the crack and nudging it open.

The bed was empty, but the rocking chair was not and her friend sat, baby Colin close, as she nursed her son, her arm perched on a collection of pillows to support his position.

Rose put a finger to her lips, but her expression held no joy. "We've had. . .a trying afternoon."

In the dim light allowed by the setting sun, Ellie sensed a darkness within her friend, and the only possible reason for it came to her. She hurried across the room and knelt at her friend's feet. "You heard from Robert."

Rose reached over Colin's body and squeezed Ellie's hand. "No. Not from him. From—"

Ellie went up on her knees and hugged her friend as best she could. Rose's shoulders heaved once, twice, before the tears dripped down her cheeks, wetting Ellie's face as well. Baby Colin's snuffles punctuated the moment, the irony of his life in the face of Robert's death not lost on her. She would do all she could to be there for her friend, just as Rose had been there for her all these months.

When her tortured knees could not stand being pressed into the hardwood another minute, she leaned back to give Rose some room to tend Colin. "Tell me about it."

Rose's lips trembled, and she stroked the back of her hand against Colin's cheek. "They think he went out onto the field to a fallen soldier and got caught in cross fire. They said he was still alive when they got to him but died later of infection."

How she hated the war. All it had taken from her. And now Rose, too, would suffer the pain and grief of loss. She stood and lifted baby Colin close to her as Rose went to the basin and splashed water into it. "Why don't you lay down and rest. I can take care of Colin."

Rose wrung out a cloth and pressed it to her face. "I don't think I could sleep, but I would like some time to myself." Her eyes softened when she stared down into her son's face. "He'll be hungry again in an hour or two."

"We'll manage, Rose. I'll take good care of him, and I'll be here tonight for you."

Rose gave Ellie a smile full of shadow and grief and sat down again in the rocking chair. "Thank you, my friend." From the table beside her, she pulled a black book onto her lap, and Ellie retreated with her small bundle, hoping Rose could find the comfort she sought in her Bible.

❧

Another crash of cannon. Another scream. A man raced toward Theo, and his gun belched a cloud of dark gray smoke. He watched as the brown-clothed man twisted, face contorted, hand to his gut where oily red liquid already pumped through his fingers. His plunge to the earth was a slow buckling of knees and twisting of the upper body, and Theo watched in morbid fascination.

"Get up! Get up!" his fellow soldier yelled in his ear. "Go! Go!"

He stood, tripped, and went down on one knee. His hand reached out for balance and touched the body of the enemy he'd just shot. The dark eyes stared at him, his lips moved, but Theo could understand nothing. Do nothing. He was the enemy and had to be conquered. The boy's lips continued to move, and his tongue darted out to lick his lips.

"Get up!" He heard the command, yet he was rooted to the spot, to the face of the first soldier he had shot. And as the seconds ticked, he watched the lips still and the man's gaze grow unfocused.

Theo opened his eyes to the stillness of the barn. He shoved himself upright, bent a knee, and rested his forearm across it, massaging his head, touching the sheen of sweat there. The same dream. He would never forget that face. Those staring eyes. The guilt that weighted him. Images of a mother waiting for her son flipped back to that pair of staring eyes. The images collided and repeated, tormenting him.

A waking torrent of war-torn memories. His friends. The smell of fear. Dismembered corpses. Bodies flying into the air upon impact and landing like the lost rag dolls of an errant child. And Bud. Always Bud. His charge forward that day in battle, a shot, then the fading warmth of Bud's hand in his as life seeped from his body. Another casualty. Another friend dead.

Sweat beaded on Theo's forehead, and he leaned forward and cradled his head in his hands. His breathing went rapid. He tugged at his hair, the pain grounding him, pulling him back to reality, even as he felt entrenched in another world where darkness ruled. The images tore at him. Accusing. Building desperation.

He hummed a hymn, but the thoughts battered him. He sang louder, thinking each word before he sang it. After one verse and chorus, the song left him, and he leaned his head back and tried to suck air into his lungs in measured breaths. To blank his mind. *Lord. Lord, help me!*

He forced himself to focus on the bits of scripture he'd heard throughout his life. "Think on these things." What were those things? Peace? Peace, yes. Joy. Love. A sound mind.

God, help me.

"Casting down imaginations, and every high thing that exalteth itself against the knowledge of God." He couldn't remember it all, but the words etched a deep path in his tortured mind. Those things that exalt against God.

God was all powerful. Even in the mind. But peace came only from a clear conscience. Why hadn't he thought to ask forgiveness for his sins? To set them at the Lord's nail-scarred feet.

His chest heaved and his mind groped for the words, but he could not utter them. They twisted and lodged in his throat. Theo doubled over in a ball.

I didn't want to do it, God. I killed him. Oh, God. Oh, God, forgive me. He pressed his hand to his mouth, his mind frenzied now to be free of the burden. His prayer eased him with each syllable, and when he cleared his mind of all the words, his declaration of freedom, the peace did come. Sweet. And pure. And joyous.

twenty-seven

In early afternoon, Ellie finally felt comfortable leaving her grieving friend. Rose had not cried again, and she'd gone about taking care of little Colin and busying herself with laundry. They talked of Robert's clothing, and Ellie urged her not to make too hasty a decision.

"Nonsense, Theo can use the clothes. Robert won't be back anyway."

So she took the clothes, noting that Rose held back a couple of shirts and the tears that flooded her friend's eyes despite her matter-of-fact words.

Rose swiped a hand down her left cheek then turned to face her. "Are you going out there today?" Rose asked later. "You should, you know. He'll miss you."

Ellie bristled. "I don't think so."

"Has he kissed you yet?"

She gasped at her friend's straightforward question. "Why—" The protest was on her tongue before she remembered the look in Theo's eyes and the warmth of his lips.

"Ah. . ." Rose breathed. "Well, good!" Her friend sent her a huge smile and headed out into the second-story hallway. "I thought it might happen soon."

Chagrined at Rose's ability to read her so well, Ellie frowned and followed her down the steps. "Honestly, Rose."

"It's putting the pink into your cheeks and the shine back into your eyes. Why fight what you're feeling?"

Rose moved into the kitchen where a small pile of linens lay on the table. Ellie plucked one up and smoothed the fabric, considering her response. "It makes me feel unfaithful."

"To what? A vow that shattered as soon as Martin drew his last breath?"

Rose's words seemed so harsh. Yet Ellie could no longer deny the truth of them. Martin was not coming back to her. Holding on to his memory was like trying to hold a rainbow in the palm of her hand. Impossible.

"Do you feel that way?" she dared to ask. Boldly assured that Rose wouldn't be able to agree with her own words once they were turned back on her.

A shadow passed over Rose's expression, and she closed her eyes. Ellie didn't know if her friend prayed in that moment or simply made up her mind, but a smile quirked along her lips, and when she opened her eyes, relief shone in her eyes. "Yes," she breathed. "Yes, Ellie, I do."

Ellie flinched.

"You're surprised." Rose lifted a stack of dried linens into her arms, and Ellie did the same with the other stack, following her friend upstairs. "Did you think what I said was somehow easier for you than for myself? I've had these months to consider that Robert might not return, and though I'll miss him and grieve for him, he would want Colin to know a father and for me to love again. I'm not ready for that now, but neither do I believe that God wants us to bog down in our grief. To love and be loved by another is His gift to us."

As Ellie left Rose to rest, she crossed to the stable, considering her friend's words. She stopped at the iron gate and removed the latch that had held it open. Open gate meant all was a go, and Martha would have seen and interpreted the silent message long before now. She would let Theo know it was safe for him to come into town later that night. He would go to Martha's, and should anyone ask, his fingers would be a good excuse. Martha would probably change his bandage just to lend credence to the excuse.

Ellie saddled the dappled gray and mounted, picking up

the reins and heading out to the farm to deliver the message and check on Theo's progress. She couldn't stay long, though, for she knew Uncle Ross would be back at some point in the evening, and she didn't want to miss the opportunity to let him know her decision. Between Martin's letters, her uncle's odd behavior, and the risk Theo endured getting to her—not to mention his friendship with Martin—she had chosen to believe his version of the story. Though she still struggled to reconcile the uncle she had known as a youth with that of a man capable of murdering her husband.

Her mind tripped over that part of the revelation. Why would he kill Martin? What did it matter whether Martin lived or died? Was there a private problem between them that Martin couldn't, or wouldn't talk about? And was it wise to confront her uncle with the truth?

Ellie sighed. It seemed a foolish thing to tell her uncle about Theo seeing him kill without some form of protection. Maybe it was best not to mention it at all, but to tell her uncle firmly and with resolve that she was not selling the farm to him and that she did not need him to help her with managing the property, or anything else for that matter. Her mother had not trained her to be coddled and dependent on a man anyway, and she didn't plan on beginning now.

Then there were Rose's words to consider. The deeper truth of what her friend was encouraging her to do. That she needed to move on from her grief for her own well-being.

Even now, she felt that swell of love for Martin, but its edges were blurred by time, like an old friend she hadn't seen for a long time whose face took a few minutes to process before recognition. In her heart, she realized she was letting go. It was the promise that time would heal grief, blur the line, and dull the edge of the pain.

She felt lighter. Free. She smiled at the image of Theo before he had kissed her. Why had she been reluctant? Hadn't she felt a pull toward him since finding him in the cellar? An attraction she tried to outrun at every turn but couldn't.

His desertion troubled her, though. Martin's talk of such things, coupled with Theo's stories, had swelled a sympathetic understanding within her, yet other men endured and even returned to their families honorably. Could she love a man who deserted the ideals he fought for, or had they never really been his in the first place? Did he, like so many, fight because of the conscription or because, like many others, he felt a need to defend his home and family from an idea contrary to his own?

Martin believed that the South should have stayed with the North and not seceded. He believed in the right of a state to govern itself but within the guidelines offered by a government unifying those ideas. Yet he, too, had struggled with the war, the death and fighting. Could she, then, fault Theo? Did his desertion make him a coward?

As she guided the horse onto the road leading to the barn, she struggled with that question the most.

❧

The springhouse squatted at the edge of the woods, a small pool of cool water surrounding it. Inside, Theo found nothing to trace the presence of the runaway couple. He used the chill water to bathe then dressed again, soaking in the peacefulness of the spot and the seclusion the small house offered from the main house and barn, though he could catch the back of that structure through a row of evergreens. The small house was the perfect place for the runaways to hide. It chilled him to think the people moved so quietly as to be untraceable. Like ghosts. He only hoped the woman had borne the move well.

He had decided to stay in the barn, what with another group needing the springhouse that night. But the roof needed a patch, and he intended on working on that and rehanging the door to make it square. He needed the work to keep him busy and his mind occupied and away from the tormenting dreams of the previous night.

Making a mental note of the supplies he would need for the repairs, he returned to the barn to gather everything, feeling refreshed in body. He would have to purchase a washbasin and stand soon. Not that he'd be here that long. . .or would he?

One day at a time.

He worked on the springhouse until he deemed himself far enough along in the repairs that he deserved a break. The air had picked up a deep chill, and Theo wished for a coat of some sort. He ran his fingers through his hair and took one more look around the springhouse, satisfied at what he had accomplished.

He swung the springhouse door shut behind him and it groaned a protest. The latch didn't set right. Theo gave the door a good wiggle to set the latch in place then froze. He thought he'd heard a branch snap and turned to stare behind him. Nothing moved. Probably a deer or some other animal wandering the woods.

Another snapping sound and he jerked his head to follow the direction from which it came. He could see nothing, but waited, still, his heartbeat racing. When his stomach clenched in panic and his mind flashed a panicked message to run, Theo steeled himself to calm. He clenched his jaw hard. When the silence stretched long, he relaxed his muscles and breathed deeply, praying for strength and peace. He had no need to be so tense over an animal.

As he started out on the path that led back to the barn, he paused when he thought he heard a horse blow air through its lips, but the sound didn't come again.

Dismissing what he heard as the wind in the trees, he set out down the path again.

twenty-eight

When Theo broke into the clearing before reaching the barn, he spotted the dappled gray nose-to-nose with Libby, the paddock fence separating them. He couldn't help but grin, and when he ducked into the barn and saw Ellie sitting on a hay bale, the sight of her stumbled the beat of his heart. "You missed me." He went to where she sat and drew her to her feet, gratified to see the sparkle of humor in her gaze.

"I came to check on my handyman and make sure he was earning his keep."

He cupped her elbows with his hands. "Sure am, boss." He wanted so much to draw her close but knew he needed to bide his time and give her a chance to let go of Martin in order to embrace whatever might develop between them. "I worked on patching that roof on the springhouse. Just need to square the door." He took a deliberate step back.

Was that disappointment in her expression? "Oh."

"Should have it done by tonight."

"Oh." She bent to pluck out a strand of hay and began to weave it through her fingers.

"Is everything a go for tonight?"

Her eyes flicked to his. "Yes. Yes, it is. I'd forgotten about that."

He motioned for her to follow him outside. "You look like you have other things on your mind." There. He'd opened the door for her to share what she was thinking. He congratulated himself for his genius.

"Rose got notice that her husband is dead."

His mind rebelled at the news. "He was a doctor."

"Yes."

He laid hold on a bag of sand and shouldered it, feeling sorrow for yet another war widow. "I'm sorry for her and for her son." His eyes traveled over her face. "And you. It must bring it all back."

She lowered her hands, eyes wide. "That's the amazing part. Rose is doing so much better than I did."

He lowered the sand to the ground and went back for another, brushing his hands together. "Everyone handles things differently."

She began weaving the straw again. "But I. . .Rose is at peace with Robert's death."

"I'm sure she will still have her moments."

"She said she's had all this time to deal with it."

"You seem to be doing fine."

❧

Ellie pursed her lips, frustrated at her inability to express herself. "I thought I was until—" She shot a glance at him, biting down on the rest of her sentence.

He lifted another bag of sand, and she admired the stretch of Martin's shirt across his back.

A blush heated her cheeks, and she looked toward the road, the fields, anywhere but at him.

She heard his grunt as he lowered the bag. "You were saying?"

There was no reason not to let him know. Not if she hoped to move on. She raised her chin and looked him straight in the face where he leaned against the back of the wagon, poised to lift another bag. "Until you came along."

"Oh?" His eyebrows lifted, and his smile showed exactly how pleased he was at her words.

"No need to be so cocky about it."

His laugh flowed as rich and deep as garden soil.

She crossed her arms and frowned.

He laughed harder.

"Honestly, Theo. It's not like I've asked you to court me." She felt the heat of her blush. Why did she have to say it like *that*? And why was he still laughing? She glared.

He caught her expression and cleared his throat. "No, ma'am, you didn't." He allowed his Southern drawl to draw out the words, and the warmth in the accent brought about a shiver of delight. "I would never expect a lady to do a man's job."

He advanced a step, his gaze locking on her, suddenly intense. When he came to stand in front of her, he blocked the low-slung sun.

She shivered again.

"Are you cold?"

She wanted to look away but couldn't. She opened her mouth to say no, but nothing came out. Those gray eyes held her captive. He touched her elbows, with a touch as gentle as butterfly wings. "Would you consider courting, Ellie?"

She was on the precipice. A tug for the old life made her afraid. Yet wasn't it that very fear that kept dragging her away from the promise of a new life? With Theo? She knew that being physically drawn to him wasn't enough, and the old question of his desertion nagged at her. But weighed against what she'd seen of him, his desertion seemed warranted.

Even while dealing with the sick soldiers, she'd come across those who wanted a reason to go home, going so far as to beg the doctor not to send them back. Could she fault Theo for deserting a cause he didn't believe in? After all he had suffered? The mental stress of watching those around him die. She bit her lip. "I need some time."

His gaze didn't waver, though his hands slid to her upper arms then fell away. "Don't wait too long, Ellie. The boss only gave me two weeks."

She thought he might laugh, but his eyes remained sober, and when he turned away, she could only watch as he shouldered the last bag of sand from the wagon. Regret washed over her.

twenty-nine

As he piled the last bag of sand upon the others, he realized Ellie had moved toward the paddock where the dappled gray stood, still saddled.

He bit down on his disappointment and frustration and went to her. As she turned the gray, she gasped when she almost plowed into his chest. Her eyes told the tale of unshed tears, and he felt a fist squeeze in his chest. As hard as her answer was for him to hear, he had to remember this was even harder for her. Her grief a territory she had never navigated before, and he could not push her. He touched her cheek. "Don't cry, Ellie."

"It's just—"

"It's all right."

She leaned her forehead against his chest.

He reached down the length of her arm to where the gray's reins were fisted in her hand. She surrendered them to his grasp.

"Why don't we talk about it later."

"But I want this. I want to—to. . ."

He pulled back slightly and dipped his head to catch her gaze. "Listen to me. You've been through a lot. I shouldn't have pushed so hard." But the words that came from his mouth weren't the ones that burned in his head.

"I didn't mean it about those two weeks, Theo." She tilted her head back. "I didn't. If you'll take your vow here, everything will work out. People would understand better why you. . .left."

Theo closed his eyes, fully understanding her hesitation now. It made sense. He was a deserter. Martin was killed in the line of duty. Or so she had thought. Even though Martin's letters had hinted at his desire to leave his regiment, he hadn't. All that mattered to her was that he look respectable to those not fighting and wondering why he had abandoned that for which he fought. And if he took his vow for the North, honor would force him to return to fight for his new allegiance.

Slow dread ate at his insides. *Lord, I thought I had settled this.*

The horrors of war. Bud. Images spiraled against his senses and flashed through his mind. They tumbled one after another. The man he had shot. Staring. The flash of gunfire. Smoke. So much smoke. It filled his lungs. . . .

Theo released his hold on Ellie and lowered his head, taking deep gulps of air, yet feeling as if all the air was being squeezed from him.

❧

Ellie saw his reaction unfold in front of her. He went pale and squeezed his eyes shut, and she feared he might fall. She pulled the reins from his hand and loosely turned the horse and tied him. When she returned to Theo, his lips moved. "Theo?"

He opened his eyes. His gray eyes were dull, filled with shadows she did not understand. "Why don't you sit down?"

He shook his head.

Ellie pressed her hand against his chest and tried to back him up. "On the wagon."

He pressed his hand over hers. "Give me a minute."

She licked her lips, afraid of what she was seeing and realizing now that she had seen him like this before. "I should get Martha to look at you."

"No." The syllable was emphatic. He squeezed her hand and closed his eyes again. His chest heaved as he took deep breaths.

She waited, helpless, for him to release her or for him to explain. He swayed, and she caught his arm with her other hand to steady him. "Theo, Please!" She began pressing at him frantically. "Please sit down."

As if pulled from a daze, he finally turned.

She followed close on his heels to make certain he reached the wagon without falling.

He patted the place next to him, not looking at her, seemingly caught on a plane of thought she couldn't comprehend.

She waited in silence, feeling every breath he took and watching as he wiped the sweat from his brow. It was like he was caught in a nightmare even though he was awake and able to walk. She recalled something else, too, the soldiers in the hospitals.

She'd been assigned to twelve soldiers inside a room at the Foster home, which had been turned into a hospital. Between the festering wounds and the groans of the three men who were closer to death than the others, she had witnessed a young soldier crying, lost in a world of horrors that caused him to break out in a sweat. The doctor called it nervousness. Effects of the war on those with no constitution. Ellie hadn't thought much of it at the time, though she remembered feeling empathy for the young man.

But now, seeing Theo, she knew he suffered, too. She put her hand over his and watched his profile for signs of the distress.

"I thought I was better after last night."

"Last night?" She traced his long fingers with her own.

"I dreamed," he said simply.

"Of what?"

He sucked air into his lungs, chest heaving with the effort. "Memories."

She waited. If he wanted to share, she would listen. If not, she would be patient.

"I killed someone."

The irony of his statement puzzled her. He'd been a soldier. Of course he had killed.

He glanced at her, studying her face, then looked away. "It was my first time. He was young. Like me." He breathed a shuddering breath that showed his struggle for composure.

She picked his hand up and nested it between both of hers. His fingers were chilled to match the cold air, but she had a feeling this coldness emanated from deep within his soul.

"I watched him. . .die."

It came to her lips to tell him she had watched wounded soldiers die and could understand, but she hadn't been the one to shoot any of them. That would be the difference.

His head dipped, and he tugged his hand from hers and put both to his face. "I asked God to forgive me."

If his reaction to shooting one man was so severe, knowing he killed so many must eat at him like a canker. "God is good and forgiving, Theo. It's yourself you need to forgive."

His hunched shoulders curled more. "If I take a vow, they'll want me to go back." She placed her hand along his back, feeling the vibration of his emotion, and the weight of what she had suggested as a solution crashed on her like the trunk of a felled tree. Taking his vow for the North and going back into the war might not kill him physically but it would mentally. Her heart broke for him, for his struggle to do what was expected of him beyond the limits of his endurance.

As his shoulders continued to shudder, she bowed her head and breathed a prayer for a healing that had nothing to do with the body or soul.

thirty

Ellie stayed with him, talking quietly, until the haunting images blurred. On occasion she swiped the hair back from his brow or her expression showed empathy as he talked. She talked, too, about a man she had seen while tending the wounded. And how that man's struggles seemed to fall along the same lines as Theo's.

He didn't feel as alone as before.

He gathered the nails, and she walked with him to the springhouse. She seemed pleased with what he had done and listened as he pointed out how he would square the door.

It was on the walk back that he realized he felt much more settled. He lost himself for a moment in the breath of chill air on his face and the new strength he felt. He raised his hands and stretched the fingers then clenched them. They were steady.

At the paddock, he cupped his hands to receive her foot as she mounted the gray. He felt her gaze heavy on him and assured her he was better. And when she turned the horse, she raised her hand in a simple gesture of good-bye.

The work on the springhouse soothed him, yet the panic that had gripped him in Ellie's presence lessened the peace he had wrapped himself in the night before. Maybe Ellie was right. Maybe God was using her to show him his need to forgive himself. He had done what was expected of him. He'd hated it, but the deed was done.

He finished squaring the door in fifteen minutes then he hitched the horse to the wagon and replaced the false bottom, piling the lumber on top. He would unload some of the wood into Ellie's barn since the porch needed repairs. The rest would do its job concealing its secret.

Theo inhaled the bracing cold air, snuggling deeper into the heavy flannel shirt Ellie had given him. The fields on either side remained stark and brown, a tribute to those who had died. A good place for horses. He could train horses again. Find a place like this and settle down to work with the majestic animals as he had in the South, before the war.

Snow would soon cover the scars of these war-torn fields. One house to his left and in the distance had been burned nearly to the ground. Another farmhouse showed severe damage to the roof. With the reminder of war came the images, but this time he forced himself to pray, and his thoughts turned to Ellie and the danger that lay ahead in transferring the eight runaways out to the farm. Maybe helping to save their lives and get them to freedom would heal him.

⁂

As Ellie came from the barn, Uncle Ross was guiding his horse down the road toward her house. Her heart began to pound as she took in his dress uniform and austere demeanor. She wondered how her news would settle with him. Not well, that was sure, but then why did she care? If he had shot Martin, she certainly owed him nothing. He halted his horse and dismounted with regal grace.

Anger-pumped blood pounded into her ears. She forced herself to be calm as he approached, a wide smile curving his lips.

"My dear niece. Let's go inside before the chill turns into a biting cold." He raised his hands to his mouth and cradled one as he blew on a clenched fist, giving imagery to his words. Ellie didn't budge. "My answer is no, Uncle Ross."

His dark eyes snapped, and his lips withered to a cruel line. "That's not the kindhearted niece I recall."

She knew the folly of showing her hand, but the words were

out before her mind could snap down on them. "You shot Martin."

Ross's expression revealed nothing. No surprise. No shock. Not even anger. Seconds passed before he raised his eyebrows. "That's quite an accusation, my dear. You know Martin died at the hands of the enemy." But his explanation was too calm.

"Why don't we go inside?" Before she could refuse, he grasped her upper arm and propelled her toward the house. "I'll go over everything I know about Martin's death, but I can't abide this cold another minute. It's the least you can do for your uncle."

She tried to pull out of his grasp, to lock her knees and free herself, but he was moving too fast and his greater weight left her no chance to assert herself. At the step leading to the back porch, she hooked her arm around a log supporting the overhang. Her arm ripped free of his grasp in a painful jarring that forced a groan from her lips. "Get off my property."

Uncle Ross faced her, his face a mask of granite coldness. "I think we should talk, Ellie, or I might just be tempted to let the authorities know about your harboring runaways."

She gasped, too late realizing that her reaction made denying his words futile.

But her uncle wasn't finished. A wan smile brushed his lips. "Perhaps you should ask your hired help about that night. I saw him with Martin."

Ellie processed the implication of what he was revealing.

"They talked for a long time and there was a lot of shouting going on. It was when Martin was leaving that your hired man shot him in the back. His own cousin."

Whatever air she had left in her lungs squeezed out and left her unable to draw another breath.

"I'm surprised you would believe a Rebel over your own flesh and blood. Your mother would be very disappointed in you."

Ellie fisted the material of her dress, glad for the support of the porch post and railing. She felt confused by the twist with which her uncle delivered the sequence of events. Theo pulled the trigger? Then it was all a lie. His journey here to tell her the truth wasn't because he felt such an obligation to her for Martin's sake.

"You should know better than to place your trust so blithely. Which is the very reason I have offered to take over your financial obligations. It is such a stress on a woman without a husband to guide her."

He kept talking. Every word beat at her mind until her thoughts became a jumble of his words mixed with memories. Theo's long journey. His sincerity. The plague that preyed upon his mind that she had suffered with him that afternoon. Their kiss. Martin's letters. His suspicions about Uncle Ross. . .

She weighed it all against what her uncle was posing as truth and realized she believed Theo and Martin more than she did Uncle Ross.

". . .it would be my honor, Ellie, to be near you."

Hadn't she seen the coldness in his eyes? Sensed that beneath the warm exterior he could put on and take off at will, there lurked a dark side? It had been what kept her from yielding to his desire to go inside and have the conversation. She feared him.

Shielding the runaways could get her into trouble, sure, but after tonight she would let Martha know of the danger and another route would be chosen for a period of time.

Her decision made, she stiffened her spine and raised her chin. "I don't need your help, Uncle Ross. My decision is final."

thirty-one

Uncle Ross took a threatening step forward, and Ellie raised her hands against whatever ill he had in mind.

"You can't talk to me like that, you little tramp. How long has that Rebel trash been hounding you? Wooing you. Don't think I haven't noticed the way you look at him." He grabbed her upper arms in a vise grip.

She cried out and began thrashing to break his hold.

"Let her go, Ross."

His hands left her arms and he spun.

Rose stood there, the black eye of the shotgun an extension of her arm.

Ross snarled and leaped off the porch. In seconds he untied the horse and worked him into a gallop before leaping into the saddle.

Ellie's knees buckled and smacked the hard boards of the porch.

Rose knelt beside her, drawing her cold hands into her own. "Can you stand?"

At first Ellie didn't think she could—the enormity of what she'd just done, the decision she had made, and the heat of Ross's rage drained her of all strength.

"I heard everything, Ellie. I reasoned that he had been badgering you about this for a long time."

She gave a weak nod.

"Just watching his expressions gave me chills, and I knew if it came down to it, I would have to help."

Ellie sighed and reached for her friend. "Thank you, Rose. Now"—she forced a smile—"help me up."

154

Rose stared at a point beyond Ellie then down at her. "Stay right where you are. I think your hero has arrived. A little late, maybe, but. . ."

Ellie blinked, not understanding until she heard the creak and jangle of a wagon. Theo. "I am not going to let him see me—" She gripped the post to pull herself upward, chagrined at the weakness in her legs. Within seconds she heard footsteps echo on the porch then felt strong hands lifting her from behind.

She was turned in the circle of Theo's arms, and his hand rose to cup the back of her head. "Ellie?"

With a deep sigh, she leaned into him. Maybe Rose was right after all. She inhaled the scent of him, closed her eyes, and let his strength be hers.

❧

Theo had been terrified to see her on her knees, instinctively knowing this was not a casual position to share a chat with Rose. Not out in the cold air.

Over Ellie's head, he swept Rose's form to reassure himself she was unhurt, a jolt tripping his heart when he caught sight of the gun she held, partially covered by the gingham of her skirts.

Rose caught the direction of his gaze and lifted it with a little laugh. "Her uncle got demanding. He needed some encouragement when Ellie invited him to leave."

Theo couldn't help a grin. So much for his idea that Rose was a dainty little woman who wouldn't think of harming anyone. The delicate weight in his arms redirected his attention. He bent his head and whispered in Ellie's ear, "Let's get inside."

Rose led the way for them. She set the gun down and put a kettle on.

Ellie pulled from his embrace and took a seat at the small table with a deep sigh.

"I'm going to check on Colin," Rose said. "I'll be back."

Theo watched Rose leave, a gust of wind blowing in from the open doorway as she slipped outside. He slid down into the seat across from Ellie.

A bit of color had flushed back into her cheeks, and she smoothed a hand over her breezed-mussed hair.

"Feeling better?" He chafed at the simple question when all he really wanted to do was gather her close and bury his face in her blond curls.

"He got so angry, Theo. He tried to tell me you had shot Martin, that you were telling me the lies." She lowered her hands from her hair and ran a hand over the smooth surface of the table. "But I knew it couldn't be true. Martin wouldn't lie to me." She searched his face. "And I knew you wouldn't lie to me either."

He gave her a brief smile that did nothing to express the warmth that he felt in that moment. She trusted him. He would hold that trust close and cherish it always.

Silence grew between them.

He raised his arm and reached across the table. She met his hand and held it firmly in her own. "I thank you for your faith in me, ma'am."

"He knows about what I do."

Fear gripped Theo hard. "Can we change the plans?"

"It's too late now. But if he's watching me. . ." She pulled in a breath. "It might be best for you to go alone this time."

He nodded. "I'll do what I can to help."

She dropped her eyes, and when she lifted her face, tears glistened there. "Is now a good time to tell you I think I'm falling in love with you?"

Theo absorbed her words like dry ground soaked in rain, but he couldn't help but tease. "You think?"

She gave him a nervous little laugh. He wouldn't release his hold on her gaze and watched the effects of the moment trace a path of red hot heat up her neck and into her cheeks.

The kettle began to sputter, prelude to a full whistle, and neither of them moved to tend to it.

She brushed her thumb across the tender place on the back of his hand where the thumb and index finger met. The gentle gesture alone expressed more to him than her words.

A knock on the door sounded, and Rose let herself in with a rush of skirts and cold air. "It's really going to be cold tonight." She took off her outerwear and hung it by the door. The kettle gave vent to a full whistle.

Theo sent a wink at Ellie and pulled his hand away. "I think I'll go unload some of the wood into the barn. I could use some cold air."

Rose turned from the stove, kettle in hand, her gaze bouncing between the two of them, a knowing smile on her lips.

thirty-two

Theo made the trip to Martha's alone. Martha greeted him with the same glint in her eyes that made him wary. "I'll not have you set foot in this house at this hour. If you want me to look at that finger, you hug into that shirt and wait. I doubt a big man like you will freeze to death."

Theo didn't have a chance to reply before she shut the door in his face. "Yes, ma'am," he mocked. "I'll surely do just that." He collapsed in the chair on the porch and wondered, again, at how eight runaways expected to fit into the tiny cavern under the false floor of the wagon.

Martha reappeared with a lantern, her features devoid of emotion. He held out his hand and she began. With two snips of the scissors, she cut away the bandage and examined the injury. "You've been working too much. The swelling will not go down if you continue to use the hand."

He wasn't sure if she expected an answer or not, so he chose to remain silent.

She went back inside, and he examined the broken joint, wondering how he could make repairs for Ellie and rest his hand. He heaved a breath and sat back in the chair, hunching his shoulders against the cold air. He would be a block of ice by the time he reached the farm.

Martha returned with a mortar and pestle, the familiar paste of a poultice within. She lifted her face to where the moon shone down on the town. "It is warmer tonight," she mumbled. He almost laughed out loud. "I was thinking how cold it was."

Martha settled herself into the chair opposite him and set the poultice on a low table that separated them. "It is cold because you are used to heat."

Her words jolted him. Yet when he caught her gaze, her expression revealed nothing. He wondered if Ellie had told Martha he was a Rebel deserter. Or maybe the woman knew by intuition; she seemed the type to be able to figure out such things.

When she finished wrapping his finger back up, she gave him a silent nod and picked up the lantern.

Knowing he was being dismissed, Theo returned to the wagon and pulled himself onto the seat. When Libby started out, he thought he could feel her straining more than normal against the harness, until momentum relieved her of some of the work.

It seemed to take forever to get down the street, turn, and reach the outskirts of town, where the fields and rolling hills dotted with trees rolled south toward Baltimore. He did his best to remain alert and the cold helped. He laughed now at Martha's easy comment, sure the woman didn't care one bit who he was, only that he had a heart to help.

As he pulled onto the lane leading to the barn, he realized that he couldn't remember any of the last twenty minutes of the journey. A strange feeling of lost time. Shaking himself, he set the brake and got down.

The silence of the night was broken by the whinny of a horse. He stared at Libby but knew it hadn't come from her. Alert now, Theo watched Libby. She turned her head, nostrils flared just as a lone rider cantered up the lane. Before Theo could move away from the wagon to put himself between the wagon and rider, he saw the flash of something in the rider's hand.

Everything seemed to happen in slow motion. A pulse of pain and a slow burn that increased in intensity made him cup his shoulder. His hand felt wetness. His mind worked to catch up as the rider flew to the ground.

The pain grew in intensity, and Theo never understood how he came to be on the ground, but he saw a face over him, backlit by moonlight, though the silver hair seemed familiar somehow.

۩

Theo jerked awake, the face of Captain Ross Bradington flooding his mind and bringing everything into sharp focus. The sway of the wagon let him know they were going somewhere. He tried to sit up, but several pieces of wood pinned him down. Theo flexed against the logs and grunted at the pain that radiated along his chest, up his neck, and down his arm. He panted, trying to catch a breath that didn't add to the pain, but every inhalation became tortuous. His head throbbed and his stomach heaved. Darkness tinged the edges of his world, and he closed his eyes to rest.

In seconds, he was alert again. The runaways! Ross was driving the wagon full of runaways. He sucked in air as best he could and braced himself against a log. It fell away, but three others blocked his ability to move.

The jostling of the wagon made his movements awkward. When the next log rolled against the side of the wagon, he could move his arms and see the back of Ross's head, but his feet were stuck beneath another log. He sat up to free his feet of the log that lay diagonally from his left thigh to his right ankle, when the wagon jolted to a stop. Theo caught sight of Ross and the cold eye of the gun aimed at his chest.

"Don't move or I'll kill you. Might kill you anyhow with all the lies you've spread."

Beside Ross sat a black man, but before Theo could process the man's appearance, Ross spit another threat.

"I'm taking this property you're hauling back south." His grin went ugly. "I imagine someone down there would give me a nice sum for your return as well. Then they can finish you off for me."

Theo's mind clutched for some way to divert Ross's attention. For one second, he gazed into the dark eyes of the black man beside Ross before that one turned away. With Ross's revelation of Theo's loyalty to the South, he knew the black man would be hesitant to help. He clenched his hands and realized the log that captured his feet could be used as a weapon. It wouldn't be easy to lift. Ross's gun could kill him faster than he could free the log.

Ross turned to the black man. "You get down there and pile those logs on him until he can't move an inch. When you're done, I'll check your work." His tone took on a snarl. "That way if you don't do a good job, you can stay up here in the North. Six feet under."

The black man climbed down from the wagon and circled to the back and out of Theo's line of vision. He felt the wagon lurch and knew the man had climbed up into the wagon bed. Theo watched as the black man crouched beside him, his face in profile to Ross. In that time, he pressed his hand against Theo's shoulder, though he never once glanced at him. Theo tried to interpret the man's gesture, cautious hope bringing a surge of strength. When the black man straightened, he hefted the log that had blocked Theo's legs and gouged a toe into Theo's side.

Theo saw the thrust of the big man's arms and heard Ross's cry of pain. Theo leaped to his feet and saw Ross holding his arm, his hand empty of the gun. Theo dove, the wagon seat catching him in his upper thighs, but his weight caught Ross off guard and sheer momentum threw them over the side and to the ground.

Theo's back hit first. He immediately pushed out as Ross's body came hurling toward him. A thrust with his hands and legs and Ross went sailing off to his right. Theo went to his side and kicked hard, landing a blow along Ross's thigh. The older man groaned and writhed.

Theo rolled to his feet and stood above the man. "Get up."

Ross glared up at him. His booted foot shot out to catch Theo behind the knees, but Theo expected such a tactic and flopped his full weight onto Ross's chest, knocking the wind from the man's lungs. Theo pulled back enough to land a blow on Ross's cheek, and the older man's gaze went unfocused. Ross put a hand to the ground, spent, sticky warmth pumping down his shoulder.

A rustle of movement beside him made him tense and turn. The black man stood there, holding the gun. He pointed the gun at Theo then at Ross. "Going north, mister. I ain't going back south again."

Theo raised his hands, grimacing at the pain the effort caused him. He gave a sharp exhale. "I'll take you there, but you're going to have to trust me. I'll need you to keep an eye on him."

The black man didn't answer but slowly, gradually, he pointed the gun away from Theo and straight down at Ross. "You bleedin' bad, mister."

"That's why I'll need your help."

"I'll keep the gun," the black man said.

Theo nodded, finding the man's reasoning agreeable. He knelt beside the still-dazed Ross and dragged him upward, holding his arms. His waning strength sent waves of nausea stirring in his gut. Theo stopped at the edge of the wagon bed. The black man had circled the wagon and moved in on the other side, blocking any attempt Ross might have at escape. Grateful for the support, Theo nudged Ross forward and waited to make sure he was going to listen before he retreated a few steps.

A roar sounded in his ears, and his hand went to his shoulder. He blinked to clear his vision and focused on the wagon seat. With great effort, he placed one foot in front of the other, knowing his strength was seeping away with every beat of his heart. He saw the wagon move but saw no one in the wagon seat. His gaze shifted to the black man, sitting in the bed of the wagon, the gun still trained on Ross.

"You drive." The black man's words penetrated the haze growing in Theo's head.

He grasped the side of the seat and placed his foot on the step. He flexed to pull himself into the wagon and gasped at the waves of pain as he sat. With slow movements, he lifted the reins, grateful now for the cool air. He tucked his chin to stare down at his shirt. A wide stain of blood had soaked a circle around the entire wound. He swayed on the seat. Or maybe that was the rocking of the wagon? He couldn't make sense of it all, and when he closed his eyes, he had no strength to open them again.

thirty-three

Ellie startled awake. A dream. Only a dream. But vestiges of it lingered like the unseen strands of a cobweb, unnoticeable until one walks through it.

Ellie pushed back the covers and swung her legs over the side. A mild gray glow let her know the sun had not yet risen. She brushed her hand down her long braid, trying to understand what had so startled her. A certainty. Something she needed to know.

She felt each strand of the woven braid as she replayed the confrontation on the porch. Something he had said. . . It eluded her.

Frustration gave her energy, and she attacked the unbraiding and brushing of her hair swiftly. All the while trying to understand what it was she was missing. It had been after his smooth words, when her firm no had ignited his temper and struck fear along her spine.

"You can't talk to me like that, you little tramp."

She'd been so shocked at the change in him. The baseness of his assessment of her character.

"How long has that Rebel trash been hounding you?"

Ellie gasped. Rebel trash! He knew!

Her breathing came in little gasps as she hurried to finish dressing. That was what her subconscious had been trying to warn her of. If Uncle Ross knew Theo was a Rebel, he might try to go after him. Coupled with the fact that she had revealed Theo's memory of Ross shooting Martin, her uncle might find it necessary to dispense with any risk that might get him in trouble with his superiors. Meaning Theo.

Breath squeezed from her in a little moan. She dashed to the barn, urgency driving her movements, her hem collecting the morning's dew as she ran. She saddled the gray as fast as she could, mounted, and snapped her crop against the horse's flanks.

Only when the lane to the barn came into view did she slow the horse. In the bright morning light, everything seemed eerily quiet. Her gaze slid over the wagon and the closed barn doors. When the gray rounded the wagon, her gaze fell to the ground where a wide pool of red made her blood race. She raised her head. "Theo?" She ran to the barn, and grappled a bit with the door. It swung open and she entered. "Theo?"

A lantern flickered at one end of the barn and she ran to it. A black man was standing up and another man lay in the hay, eyes closed. Theo. A wounded sound came from Ellie's throat.

The black man held up a hand. "He is asleep."

Ellie didn't recognize him. "Who are you?"

"He needs a doctor. Bad. I done all I could, but he's got the fever."

Ellie sank to her knees and pressed a hand to Theo's brow. "What happened?"

None of it made sense. The blood on the drive must have been Theo's. Ross had gotten to him. It couldn't have been the black man, or why would he care for Theo afterward?

"Am I in the North?"

Ellie turned to the man. "Yes, you are."

Relief relaxed the black man's lips, and the lines around his eyes faded. "I was afraid I was at the wrong place. The old man in the blue coat came and shot him"—he indicated Theo with his eyes—"then found us in the wagon. He was taking us south, going to get the bounty for us, but the mister here stopped him." The black man stood and motioned for Ellie to follow him.

She plucked at his sleeve, and the black man stopped. "What

about the others?" she whispered.

His teeth gleamed in the low light. "Got 'em to the place. I stayed to help the mister."

In the empty stall next to Libby's, her uncle sat on the ground, his legs and wrists bound, a cloth around his mouth. His eyes were bloodshot, and one was swollen and blackened. When he lifted his head to see who had approached, he scowled at Ellie and turned his face away.

Words wouldn't come to Ellie, and Theo's need trumped her desire to hear what her uncle had to say. She spun on her heel. "Can you help me load him in the wagon?"

The black man didn't move. "I'm safe here?"

It would be a natural worry, Ellie understood, but she needed the man's help. "If you want to stay here in Gettysburg, you can work for me. I have a lot of repairs that need to be done."

"My name's Josiah, ma'am, and I'd be grateful to work for you and the mister."

Ellie didn't bother wasting the time to explain Theo's relationship to her, not with the fever pulling strength from his body every minute it raged.

&

Martha sat on the porch, rocking in her chair, when Josiah pulled the wagon up to the house days later. Ellie allowed Josiah to help her down. Rose followed, with baby Colin bundled tightly.

Josiah turned to Ellie. "Will you be long, ma'am?"

She smiled at him. "I might. Come on in. I'm sure Martha would like to see you."

She delighted in watching the black man's obvious consternation at being found out. For all the times his face masked his emotions, it had been obvious to her from the start that Martha captured his attention. Ellie stared up at Martha who had stood and come to the edge of the porch. Seemed Martha felt the same way about Josiah.

"Josiah, you put that horse away around back. I'm guessing Miss Ellie'll want to put in a good long visit now that he's awake."

Ellie's head came up, and she gasped in surprise.

"Oh, that's wonderful news." Rose gave words to the moment.

Ellie started toward the steps, excitement lifting her spirits. It had been nearly two weeks since Theo had been awake for more than a few minutes, though Martha kept saying those few minutes were a good thing. Still, it had worried her. But now. . . "When?"

Martha led the way through the door and to the back of the house. "Just this morning I went in and noticed him stirring more than usual. About an hour later, he was wide awake and asking for something to eat. Full of questions, he was. Plumb wore me out with all the tongue waggin' he done." She opened the door to his room and rolled her eyes toward the man on the bed. "I'll be out here talkin' with Miss Rose. We needs to decide what to do now that the doctor isn't coming home."

Ellie purposely didn't look right at Theo at first. She had waited for this moment for so long. It was one thing to see him when he was unconscious, but now that he was awake and able to see her, too. . .

"Who are you?"

Her heart plummeted, and she turned toward him.

His face split in a huge smile that told her he was teasing. "I thought maybe I'd grown so ugly you couldn't stand the sight of me."

Ellie took the seat next to the bed where she'd sat for the many days he struggled through the fever then lingered in unconsciousness.

His jaw sported a few days' growth of beard, and his cheeks were hollowed from the weight he'd lost, but his eyes. . . Her breath caught at the light that glowed from his eyes.

A happy light passed over his face and grew in intensity until she felt the heat rising in her cheeks. "Really, Theo."

"I can't help it. You're a beautiful woman."

She pressed her hands to her face. "We're not even courting."

"I hope to be asked as soon as I get back on my feet."

"You lost a lot of blood."

"So I heard."

"Josiah said the only reason he found the barn was because he'd paid close attention to the road Uncle Ross used."

"Josiah?"

"The black man who helped you get back here."

"I must have passed out."

Ellie pulled at the fabric of her skirt so that it settled around her legs more comfortably. "You did. Josiah wasn't sure if he was at the right place or not."

"Your uncle Ross figured he would capture whatever slaves we were hiding then take them down south to collect the bounty. Did he confess to everything?"

Ellie pressed her lips together. "Yes. They put him under arrest."

Theo slid his hand over and waggled his fingers in invitation.

She took it, her heart full because of this man. The rough bandage rubbed against her fingers, and she lifted his bandaged middle finger for examination. "I'm sure your being unconscious has helped this heal."

"It's the least of my hurts right now."

"Still bad?"

Theo raised their clasped hands and placed hers against his chest. "This helps."

"I'm serious."

He widened his eyes. "So am I."

☙

How Theo loved to see her cheeks awash with color. Her blushes always made her eyes bluer. If she truly knew the pain that spiked along his arm and neck every time he moved his hand, she would have never allowed him to even hold her hand. But he didn't care. The pain was worth it.

"Tell me about this black man."

Ellie gave a little laugh that amused him, though he didn't quite understand her mirth. "Ask Martha. She probably knows more about him than anyone."

He couldn't believe it. "Martha? And Josiah?"

Ellie gave an enthusiastic nod. "I think so."

Theo's mind clicked along at the news. But something else troubled him. "Your uncle was spying on us, wasn't he?" He recalled the whinny of the horse he'd heard at the springhouse and when he'd been woken in the night by a sound he couldn't pinpoint. "He must have been watching my movements."

"He'd been watching you, mostly, trying to figure out your connection to me and if it went deeper than merely a hired hand. And, of course, he overheard my conversation with Martha and decided to cash in on the moment and take care of you at the same time. After shooting you, he found the slaves in the wagon, got Josiah out, and made him pick you up and put you in the wagon."

"Good thing for me. If it hadn't been for Josiah's help, I don't think things would have worked out quite as nicely." He pulled in a slow breath. "What about the runaways?"

"When Josiah got back to the barn, he told them all to go ahead as planned. They would have been a little bit behind schedule, but being in the North seemed to give them some peace of mind."

He heaved a sigh of relief. "That's good to know."

"You're getting tired."

"No, I'm fine."

"You are not."

"If I fall asleep, will you stay?"

"I have to."

He cracked his eyes open. "You have to?"

"Martha and Rose needed to talk about their plans for the office now that Robert isn't coming home."

Was she deliberately avoiding what he meant? "You sound like you don't want to stay."

Her eyes danced. "I've watched you sleep for the past nine days."

"Did you miss me?"

She tilted her head, a sparkle coming into her eyes. "Not as much as I will when you leave."

"Where am I going?"

"Well, seeing as how I need those repairs done and you're lying in here sleeping, I hired Josiah to take care of things."

"So I don't have a job then."

She shook her head, but the light danced in her eyes. "No."

"I guess I'll be leaving then as soon as I'm able."

"I guess so."

He was going to have to pry it out of her. "That makes you happy?"

She leaned forward, her breath on his cheeks. "It does because I was hoping that you would decide to stay if I offered you a promotion."

He turned his head toward her, all vestiges of sleepiness gone. "A promotion to. . . ?"

"Suitor?"

"Ellie Lester," he breathed, "are you inviting me to come courting?"

When she pressed her lips to his, he knew he had his answer.

epilogue

Dear Rose,

It has been a wonderful time. The Bedford Springs Resort is lovely, though the ride out here from the train was rough. Theo and I have enjoyed our time together so much. He has been so patient to wait so long before we wed. But I wanted to be sure. I'm sure that makes you laugh, since you were convinced far before I was. I knew I truly loved him when he agreed to risk going south to bring home Martin's body. Still, it troubles me that some view our marriage as a slap to the face, even daring to treat him—us—with such derision. I believe it helps him that Josiah, Martha, and most of the blacks view him as a hero for what he did that night. If only the white people were as convinced, but I must not judge them too harshly, for I can understand how they feel, especially those who lost their husbands and sons.

We leave here in a few days to go out to Council Bluffs, as far as the train will take us, but still plan to return on the agreed date. I hope Josiah asks Martha to marry him soon. Please make sure he gets paid. The money will help ease his mind on the matter.

I hope by now you have found someone to buy our house and that you are getting settled in with Martha. I know she is a comfort to you, just as she was a help to Robert. Give Colin a kiss for me. Tell him his Aunt Ellie will bring him a wonderful toy to play with.

Oh, and please let Josiah know that we've decided to take his idea and build a wall in the largest room on the second floor of the farmhouse. We'll need the room should we have children. Not that I'm in the family way yet, but it is one of our dreams to raise a family on the farm where I spent all my growing-up years.

Take care, my dear friend. I'll write again soon.

Love,
Ellie

A Letter To Our Readers

Dear Reader:
In order that we might better contribute to your reading
enjoyment, we would appreciate your taking a few minutes
to respond to the following questions. We welcome your
comments and read each form and letter we receive. When
completed, please return to the following:

Fiction Editor
Heartsong Presents
PO Box 719
Uhrichsville, Ohio 44683

1. Did you enjoy reading *Promise of Time* by S. Dionne Moore?
   ❑ Very much! I would like to see more books by this author!
   ❑ Moderately. I would have enjoyed it more if

   _____

   _____

   _____

2. Are you a member of **Heartsong Presents**? ❑ Yes ❑ No
   If no, where did you purchase this book? _____

   _____

3. How would you rate, on a scale from 1 (poor) to 5 (superior),
   the cover design? _____

4. On a scale from 1 (poor) to 10 (superior), please rate the
   following elements.

   ____ Heroine   ____ Plot
   ____ Hero   ____ Inspirational theme
   ____ Setting   ____ Secondary characters

5. These characters were special because? _____

_____

_____

6. How has this book inspired your life? _____

_____

_____

7. What settings would you like to see covered in future
   Heartsong Presents books? _____

_____

_____

8. What are some inspirational themes you would like to see
   treated in future books? _____

_____

_____

9. Would you be interested in reading other **Heartsong
   Presents** titles? ❑ Yes ❑ No

10. Please check your age range:

    ❑ Under 18   ❑ 18-24
    ❑ 25-34   ❑ 35-45
    ❑ 46-55   ❑ Over 55

Name _____

Occupation _____

Address _____

City, State, Zip _____

E-mail _____

JERSEY BRIDES

Issues of wealth have three Nineteenth-Century New Jersey women tied in knots, but can God use their trials to bring romance into their lives?

Historical, paperback, 352 pages, 5.1875" x 8"